WRAPPED UP IN YOU

MELODY CLAIRE

Copyright © 2023 by Melody Claire

All rights reserved.

No part of this book may be reproduced in any form or by any electronic or mechanical means, including information storage and retrieval systems, without written permission from the author, except for the use of brief quotations in a book review.

Cover Design: Kate Farlow Y'all. That Graphic.

Editing: Abbie Nicole

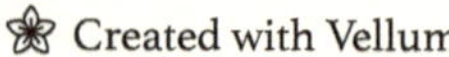 Created with Vellum

For every person with ADHD who's been told they just need to focus a little more or try a little harder...I see you.

1

JONATHAN

December 23

I swirled the bourbon in my glass, watching the amber liquid wash over the oversized cube of ice, coating the inside of the glass before sliding back down to pool at the bottom. I brought the glass to my lips and tossed back the contents in one swallow before setting the glass down on the coffee table with a thunk next to the half-empty bottle.

In front of me, flames in reds, yellows, and oranges licked at the logs I'd stacked in the fireplace an hour ago. Since then, I'd worked steadily at getting blindly drunk. Based on the warmth humming through my veins and the fuzziness in my head, I'd say I was more than halfway toward accomplishing that goal.

I picked up the bottle to pour another round—*this bourbon wasn't going to drink itself*—when the door to the tiny cabin burst open, blowing in a gust of cold air and startling the shit out of me.

The bottle slipped through my fingers as I turned in reflex to see who the intruder was. Glass shattered on the hardwood floor beneath me and liquid spread in a puddle around my feet, but I made no move to escape the mess.

"What the fuck are you doing here?"

"Good to see you too, brother." He flashed me a grin, then shook his head and stomped his feet, leaving a mess of snow on the floor around him.

"Close the damn door. Jesus. You're letting snow in, and it's making a mess."

A chill slithered up my spine as the warmth of the cabin dissipated amid this assault from the storm raging outside. Hayden, my *step*brother, turned and closed the door behind him, dropping his bags, and what was that?—a guitar?—on the floor next to the entrance. He toed off his boots and began removing his winter-weather gear, spreading snow everywhere in the process. I would need a mop to deal with the mess he was making. *Figures.*

My thoughts came to a record-scratching halt as he began removing his jeans.

In the middle of the entryway.

Right in front of me.

His thick thighs and toned calves were covered in a layer of dense dark hair. His firm ass was clad in a pair of red boxer briefs with candy canes all over them, and when he turned, I caught sight of the very prominent bulge his hoodie did nothing to hide. *Jesus.* What would it look like when he was hard?

I swallowed. That was a thought I'd never had about him.

"What are you doing?" I ground out through gritted teeth. As tipsy as I was, I wasn't nearly drunk enough for this turn of events, but as the bourbon I'd been drinking was currently soaking through my socks on the floor, I'd have to bear it in my current not-drunk-enough state.

Oblivious to the war raging inside my head and body, he paused and looked at me as if I was an idiot. "Taking off my pants."

"In the middle of the entryway?"

"Some of those snow drifts came up to my knees. And since you seemed so bothered by the mess I was making, I took them off here by the door rather than traipsing snow across the living room."

That actually made some sense. Dammit.

He returned to his production of undressing, removing his socks, making him nearly naked from the waist-down, before grabbing his duffel bag and crossing over to the single bathroom.

"Be right back." The little shit winked at me before shutting the door.

In the sudden silence of the room, I became very aware that my socks were soaked through. I looked down and sighed, dropping my chin to my chest before taking another deep breath and carefully stepping out of the puddle and away from the broken glass.

I stripped out of my socks, then found a pair of slippers and got to work cleaning up the mess as carefully as I could in my muddled state. As I worked, my thoughts turned to Hayden and what could have brought him here, especially in the midst of a blizzard. I'd left yesterday, ensuring I beat the storm the forecasters had predicted. Had Hayden even known I was up here? Probably not. He likely hadn't been aware of the storm either. The kid—*man*, I corrected myself —rarely did anything with any sort of forethought. If you looked up the definition of impulsive in the dictionary, you'd find a picture of Hayden Harrison.

Under what words would my picture reside? Anal. Boring. Predictable. Those are certainly the words Rebecca would have used. Did use. She'd flung them in my face the day she asked for a divorce six months ago.

"Why do you have to be so goddamn anal about everything, Jonathan? I can't take it. No one's allowed to make a mistake in your presence. Not a single towel out of place on the rack or a dish out of place in the dishwasher. And heaven forbid if I leave my shoes in the living room."

"Is it a sin to want things orderly?" I blustered. What was so wrong with wanting things neat?

"I'm wasting away in this marriage. We never do anything off-script. Work. Eat. Sleep. Repeat. Lasagna on Tuesdays. Dinner at the club on Saturdays. Missionary position. Every. Single. Time. It's boring, and the predictability is sucking the life out of me. I want a divorce."

Hayden came out of the bathroom, still wearing his hoodie, but his lower half was now covered in a pair of ratty old joggers riding low on his hips. The elastic was loose in one ankle and both knees were almost completely worn through, but they hugged his bulge and thighs in such a way as to almost be indecent. As someone fastidious in all his attire, the worn-out nature of the sweats should have been a turn-off, but instead, I found myself turning away from him to adjust my hard-on as discretely as I could manage. I blamed this sudden attraction on the alcohol.

I bent over and swept the last of the glass into the dishpan.

"Ow. Shit. Motherfucker." I clutched my hands to my chest, pressing my left palm across the right and applying pressure to the gash I'd just stupidly given myself. I wasn't sure whether it was the effects of the alcohol making me sloppy or Hayden's bulge causing too much of a distraction, but I'd been careless, and now my dominant hand was bleeding all over the damn place. It was already oozing from between my hands and running down my wrist.

"Jesus. Let me see it." Suddenly, Hayden was by my side, gingerly taking my hand in his to get a better look at the cut. His hands were chilly from the cold but surprisingly gentle as he lifted my right hand to examine my injury. "No idea if you need stitches, but I don't think we're going anywhere in this weather, so we better wrap it up as best we can. Do we have a first-aid kit?"

I stared at him intently, surprised at how quickly he'd gone into caretaker mode. I'd never seen him like this, though I supposed I rarely saw him much at all. I'd been twenty-four when our parents started dating, twenty-five when they married. When Hayden had graduated from high school, I'd already been several years into my first job as a corporate accountant. He'd gone off to college three states away while I'd been trying to climb the corporate ladder and find the perfect spouse. In the eight years we'd known each other, I didn't think we'd ever spent more than a day or two together, and those instances had been holidays and family gatherings when there were a lot of other people around. I honestly couldn't remember if we'd ever had a serious conversation. My perception of him had always been that he was an aimless kid with no direction who never took anything seriously. Not only were there eight years between us, but we were also seriously mismatched in personality. We had nothing in common.

When I didn't answer his question, he looked at me, eyebrows raised. The genuine concern I saw reflected in his eyes gave me pause. When was the last time anyone had looked at me with that kind of care? It filled me with warmth, even as it made me uncomfortable.

I nodded in the direction of the bathroom. "There's a kit in the cabinet under the sink."

Wordlessly, he guided me toward the bathroom and gestured for me to sit on the toilet while he searched for the first-aid supplies. He pulled out the kit and set it on the counter. Rummaging around, he produced gauze and tape and set them aside. I sucked in a breath as he carefully took my hand and brought it closer to the sink. "Sorry," he said, wincing in sympathy. "I just want to make sure there's no glass lodged in it."

I held my breath while he inspected the wound. He gave a nod, as if satisfied, then began cleaning it. His movements were gentle yet efficient as he cleaned the cut and then wrapped it with gauze. "How do you know how to dress a wound like this?" I asked as he tucked in the end of the gauze and began taping it up.

"I went through a skateboarding phase in high school. I banged the shit out of myself often enough that I learned how to dress a cut properly." I vaguely remembered a skateboard or two in the mudroom at our parents' house when they'd first started dating. I hadn't paid it any attention at the time, but I supposed those had probably been Hayden's boards.

He brought my palm to his lips and placed a soft kiss over the bandage. Our eyes caught, and he blushed. "Sorry. Habit." He released my hand and made himself busy organizing the supplies back into the first-aid kit.

"You make it a habit of kissing other people's wounds? Is this something that happens often?"

"I mean, I guess not. But Mom always did it for me. Just felt right, I guess."

"Do you always do what feels right?" It was a loaded question, but one I couldn't help asking.

"Mostly." He let out a self-deprecating chuckle. "I mean, it almost always ends badly, but I can't seem to help myself." Our eyes held, and my pulse quickened. I watched in fascination as something like heat flickered through his eyes, but it was quickly extinguished before he turned away abruptly, putting the supplies back under the sink.

We left the bathroom and crossed to the small kitchenette, where Hayden opened the fridge. "What's for dinner?" he asked, shifting things around this way and that, finally coming up with a bottle of my favorite IPA. He opened it and handed it to me before opening another for himself. I probably shouldn't drink any more tonight, but the thought of spending the evening with my flighty stepbrother while sober was incredibly unappealing.

"You never answered my question," I stated, leaning against the counter adjacent to him, sipping my beer. He was a few feet away from me, yet I could feel the heat radiating off him. If I leaned into it, would I get burned?

He eyed me as he took a long pull off the bottle, mirroring my stance, though much more relaxed. "What?"

"I asked you earlier...what are you doing here?"

"Oh." He shrugged. "I didn't have anywhere else to go."

"What's wrong with your apartment?"

"Nothing. But my roommate is proposing to his girlfriend on Christmas Eve, so he asked if I could make myself scarce."

"Your roommate is proposing to his girlfriend in your apartment?" I'd been to his apartment exactly one time. He lived in a nondescript, nine hundred-square foot, two-bedroom apartment with a guy he'd gone to college with. It was your basic bachelor situation. There wasn't a single romantic thing about it.

He took another pull on his beer and shrugged. Again.

Shrugging was basically his personality in a nutshell. "I think he was going to do a candlelit dinner kind of deal. We didn't really talk about the details."

"What about your dad? Why not spend Christmas with him?" Our parents—his mom and my dad—were spending the holidays in Jamaica, but as far as I knew, his father still lived in the city, and I thought they got along all right.

Something almost like pain crossed his features. It was a look I'd never seen on him before. I was surprised to find I didn't like it. "He, uh...we had a fight."

2

HAYDEN

"You had a fight? About what?"

"You don't want to hear about that. Why don't I work on figuring out dinner? You probably can't cook with your hand like that." I set aside my beer and began rummaging through the cabinets, assessing what we had on hand that I could put together for dinner. I didn't want to talk about the fight with my dad. The wound was an old one that had been reopened over and over again, leaving an ugly scar. This time around, it was still too fresh, too raw to bear examining further, especially with the oh-so-perfect Jonathan.

"You know how to cook?" Jonathan asked from behind me, disbelief evident in his tone. I stiffened as I grabbed some ground beef and moved over to the stove, pulling out a sauté pan and setting it on one of the burners. I was tired of the people in my life assuming I couldn't do anything. I'd played the part of the happy-go-lucky, affable son/stepbrother/best friend/roommate for so long that no one bothered to look further. But I wasn't stupid, and I wasn't helpless, and I was tired of people thinking that was the case.

"Yeah, I went through a cooking phase last year when I started working at Olive & Vine." I tried not to let his judgment get to me. I was used to it, but for some reason, it bothered me a little more coming from him. "On slow nights, I used to watch the cooks on the line. I was fascinated with the way they could have so many different things going at the same time and have everything come out perfect and on time. I wanted to learn how to do it myself."

"Really?" He sounded incredulous, and after the fight with my dad and the long drive up here in a snowstorm, I broke. I stopped in the middle of the kitchen, my hands full of boxed pasta and a jar of spaghetti sauce, and glared at him.

"Is it really so hard to believe that I might be competent at something? Just because I don't have a *career* doesn't mean I'm stupid. Or that I don't have skills." It was the same bullshit my dad spewed at me at every turn, and I was over it.

Jonathan had the presence of mind to look at least a little contrite as he sputtered, "I'm sorry. I didn't mean to offend. I was just..."

"Surprised? Yeah. I got that." I placed my items on the counter and continued to get out the rest of the things I would need for basic spaghetti and meat sauce. "If we were at home, I'd cook a real bolognese, but since you only brought stuff from a jar, this will have to do."

I got to work boiling water and browning the ground beef I'd found in the fridge. "What other hidden talents do you have?"

I flicked an eye over my shoulder, looking for lingering judgment, but his expression appeared to be one of genuine curiosity. I released a breath, attempting to let go of some of my tension. "I've tried a lot of different things over the years.

I have ADHD, so I tend to get really excited about something, hyper-focus on it for a while, and then lose interest. I've been that way my whole life, but I didn't get diagnosed until college, so I never really understood why I could never stick with just one or two things."

"What kinds of things have you tried?"

"Well, I mentioned the skateboarding thing earlier. And cooking. When I was younger, like fourth grade, I was really into Marvel comics. It's not really a skill, but at one point, I could tell you every obscure fact about the MCU but could barely add and subtract fractions. I'm good at video games, but that's not really a skill either." I got out a loaf of bread and began slicing it. "I was into photography for a while. Pilates—thought about becoming an instructor. Gardening." I shrugged. "I guess I still do all of those to some degree. But none of them held my interest enough to become a career."

"Do any of them have to lead to a career? Can they just be hobbies?"

I set the buttered bread on a cooking sheet and turned on the broiler. "Not to my father. He thinks I need to 'quit fucking around and get a real job'—his words." I popped the bread into the oven and then turned to drain the pasta.

"Are any of them things you could turn into a career?"

I didn't respond as I moved the pasta back to the stove and added the browned meat and sauce. I gave it a stir, contemplating how much I wanted to say. This was the longest conversation I could recall having with Jonathan, and it felt personal in a way I didn't get with many people. From the outside looking in, I was sure my life looked like chaos, especially to someone as precise and organized as Jonathan. I was messy, my clothes didn't always match, and I ran late for everything. I'd been a server at Olive & Vine for two years, but most didn't see that as a real career. Dad certainly hadn't. And if I was honest, though I'd enjoyed the work, it hadn't been what I wanted for myself long-term.

But could I do the thing I wanted most? The one thing in my life I'd never lost interest in? In fact, it was the only thing I'd become more passionate about as I'd gotten older. I hadn't told anyone. I was afraid that if I spoke it into the universe, I'd somehow jinx it, and then the thing I loved most would feel like another failure.

I pulled the garlic bread out of the oven and placed it on the potholder I'd gotten out. "Dinner's ready!" I said with an abundance of cheer I didn't remotely feel.

"You didn't answer my question."

"You're right. Let's eat."

Taking my hint, he dropped the topic, and we prepared plates and moved over to eat at the small table in the eating area adjacent to the kitchen. A large bank of windows overlooking the forest let in an abundance of natural light during the day, but darkness had fallen, so the only thing visible was the snow gathered around the edges of the window frames. Wind howled and buffeted the house. This storm wasn't letting up anytime soon.

We ate in silence for a bit, as if we were dancing around each other, unsure what to say. I knew almost nothing about Jonathan other than that he was a successful corporate accountant and our parents thought there was nothing he couldn't do. They'd never said it, but I knew they'd always wished I could be more like him. Driven. Ambitious. Perfect spouse. Perfect life.

I didn't know how to compete with that. I was a server. I knew how to strike up a conversation with anyone about anything. But this man, I had no idea what to say to him.

Except, where was his wife? It was the Christmas holiday. Shouldn't he be with her? She'd always struck me as a bit of a cold one, but then, Jonathan wasn't exactly warm either. They'd seemed a good enough match, but what did I know? I'd never dated anyone for any significant amount of time, so I knew fuck-all about relationships.

"So, um, why aren't you with Rebecca? I was expecting the cabin to be empty with it being the holidays and all."

He glared at me. *Shit*. Apparently, I'd struck a nerve. "If you must know, Rebecca and I are divorced."

My eyes nearly fell out of my head. I'd had no idea. "When did that happen? Do our parents know? I wouldn't have thought they'd have gone on their trip if they knew you were going to be alone."

"You're alone." He raised one eyebrow, giving me a pointed look.

I waved him off. "Yeah, but they thought I would be with my dad. Not sure it would have mattered anyway."

His gaze was assessing. "Don't be absurd. Of course it would have mattered." He stood from the table, taking his plate into the kitchen. "My divorce was finalized two days ago. And to answer your question, yes, they know. But they booked this trip nearly a year ago, and it was nonrefundable."

I was at a loss for words. "What happened? With Rebecca, I mean?" I rose from the table, following him into the kitchen with my dishes. He set his on the counter with a clank. He kept his eyes down and his back to me. He breathed deep as if pulling himself together, and I had the strangest urge to close the few feet of distance between us and put my hand on his back to offer some sort of comfort. My relationship with Jonathan had always been distant, but seeing him like this, vulnerable and hurting, struck a chord inside me I didn't want to examine too closely.

Before I could make a move, he straightened his spine and, without turning, said, "I'll take care of the dishes."

He clearly didn't want to share his shit any more than I wanted to share mine. "You probably shouldn't get that hand wet. I'll take care of the dishes."

Ignoring me, he began running water in the sink, adding soap. "Don't be ridiculous. You cooked. I'll clean up." He began adding dishes and utensils to the soapy water. I crossed the distance between us, placing my hand over his injured one to stop him. "Jonathan, don't be a stubborn ass. Let me do the damn dishes." I was pressed right up against him, my chest to his shoulder. I fought the urge to lean into his warmth, to inhale his scent, to press my lips to the curve of his neck. I'd buried those urges for eight years. I could continue to do so now.

"Fine," he gritted out. He sounded so damn angry, and I wasn't sure why, but I'd long ago given up trying to figure him out. He jerked away from me, exiting the kitchen and taking his warmth with him.

3

____

JONATHAN

I walked into the bedroom and slammed the door. I had to get away from Hayden. The feel of him pressed against me and the sound of his gruff voice as he admonished me had my dick straining against my fly to the point of pain. I hadn't been with a man in a long time, since before Rebecca. I'd forgotten how good a male body could feel against mine and how a gruff tone of voice could shoot straight to my dick. Yet even as he stirred that lust inside me, the gentle way he'd put his hand on mine to stop me while still making sure he didn't hurt me left a swirl of confusing emotions in my chest. Lusting after my stepbrother was problematic enough, but adding feelings into the mix was simply impossible. I shouldn't go there. *Couldn't* go there.

I pulled a pair of pajama pants and a clean Henley out of my bag and laid them on the bed, willing my hard-on to go down. I needed to pull myself together before I went out there. Maybe by tomorrow, the storm would have blown over, and I could head home. Hayden could have the cabin to himself, and I could put some much-needed distance between us. We could go back to being nothing more than acquaintances whose parents happened to be married.

I just had to get through tonight.

I fumbled with changing my clothes, which took twice as long due to my damn hand, setting aside my neatly folded dirty clothes to keep them from mixing with the clean ones. Smoothing my good hand through my hair, I took a breath, feeling much steadier.

I grabbed my Kindle, hoping it would be a good distraction, and walked out into the living space. The small seven hundred-square-foot cabin had been built by my grandfather nearly sixty years ago. He'd come up here to fish and hunt, so it had been built for efficiency rather than aesthetics. The building itself was a rectangle with a small galley-style kitchen, an adjacent eating area that barely held a table for two, and a tiny bedroom just large enough to hold a double bed and three-drawer dresser.

There were two features of the cabin that were my favorites. One was the bay of windows in the eating area. I loved the natural light and view of the woods they offered during the day. The second was the fireplace in the living room. It was wood-burning with a stone surround that flowed all the way up the wall, the only design feature of note in the otherwise plain wood cabin. The space held a battered braided rug, an ugly couch that was at least thirty years old, and a single recliner that listed to one side and was uncomfortable as fuck.

The fire had died down some while we were eating, but Hayden was currently bent over, attempting to bring it back to life. The sight of those ratty sweatpants stretched over his tight ass had my dick tenting my pants once again. *Goddammit.* This insanity had to stop.

I strode across the room, nudging him out of the way.

"Move and let me do it. You're going to set the whole damn place on fire."

"Ow! Jesus." He rubbed his arm where I'd nudged—okay, shoved—him, a look of irritation on his face. I probably deserved that, but I couldn't seem to get my temper under control around him. Which only made my anger flare higher. I prided myself on my ability to control my emotions, and it pissed me off that I couldn't do so around him.

I fiddled with the logs and the poker, rearranging the wood to ensure the fire would burn for a while. Satisfied, I set the poker back in its holder and turned as Hayden walked over with his guitar in hand. While I'd been messing with the fire, he must have moved one of the stools over from the breakfast bar because that's where he sat now, one foot on the ground and the other on the rung as he twisted and turned the pegs while strumming the strings.

Anger forgotten, I took a seat on the couch, crossing one ankle over the opposite knee, looking on in open curiosity. I'd vaguely noticed a guitar case when he'd arrived, but I'd been rather distracted and hadn't given it much thought. Now, as I thought back over the years, I didn't remember any mention of him playing the guitar at all. Was this another one of his phases? One of those things he got fixated on before giving up when he got distracted by something else?

He must have sensed me staring because he paused his tuning and looked at me. "This okay?" he asked.

Embarrassed at getting caught staring, I shrugged, then picked up my Kindle, hoping it could provide the distraction I was looking for. Hayden strummed a couple of times, starting and stopping as if he couldn't decide what to play. After a few moments, he seemed to settle on something and started to play, his notes filling the air and wrapping around me, and I gave up trying to concentrate and set my Kindle aside.

He was good. Really good.

I didn't know anything about playing the guitar, but I'd taken piano for years and was fairly decent—good enough to recognize talent when I heard it. He played a couple of Christmas carols, older ones I recognized but couldn't remember the names of. His fingers moved assuredly along the frets and the strings, never faltering as he moved from one song to the next. I was captivated, and I found my earlier anger dissipating as he cast a spell around me with the way he wove notes and phrases together.

"Do you sing as well?" I asked as he came to the end of one song. He hadn't glanced up at me since he started, almost as if he'd forgotten I was there, but he looked up at my question and nodded, then launched into another song.

This one I recognized. "O Holy Night" had always been one of my favorites, but as he moved past the instrumental introduction and began to sing, I was mesmerized. His voice was unlike anything I'd ever heard. His baritone was smooth, rich, and honey-sweet, weaving itself around me as he sang. And with his eyes closed and the light from the fire playing on his features, I couldn't take my eyes off him.

The melody shifted, long notes soaring as we approached the dramatic conclusion. His voice filled the cabin effortlessly, despite the shift in range, as if this song, written over a hundred years ago, was written specifically for Hayden's voice. I'd always favored the Josh Groban version, but this one, sung by Hayden in a tiny cabin in the middle of the woods, would forever replace it as my favorite.

The final chord rang through the cabin, fading until the only sound remaining was the crackle of the fire and the wind whipping around the eaves. At length, he looked up at me, a question in his eyes that I didn't have an answer for. I couldn't speak. Couldn't form words. I was absolutely stunned.

When I didn't say anything, he looked down, strumming randomly a couple of times and repositioning himself on the stool. He looked back up at me, flashing a smile, one I'd seen on him many times that I was starting to suspect wasn't entirely sincere. "Do you have any requests?"

"Hayden, that was...amazing." His face lit up at the praise, even as a flush crept up his cheeks. "How long have you been playing?"

"Thank you. Um, I begged Mom for lessons when I was in seventh grade, I think. I was relentless, asking her over and over again until she finally caved and got me a guitar and lessons for Christmas that year. It's the only thing I've ever tried that stuck."

"Your voice is..." I was still struggling to put my thoughts into words. "I've never heard anything like it. You have a gift." He ducked his head, like maybe he was uncomfortable with the praise, but I caught the turn of his lips and thought maybe he was pleased too. "How come I've never heard you play before?"

He strummed absentmindedly as he answered, as if his fingers had a mind of their own. "I don't know. I guess I didn't think anyone would want to hear me play."

"Why would you think that? You're very good." I couldn't believe this was the first time I was hearing him. I would have thought he would have played at a Christmas gathering or any number of other family events. I didn't even think I'd ever heard Dad or Suzanne mention he played. It didn't seem right that his talent had been kept locked away. It should be shared with everyone.

He shrugged. "Mom has always supported my hobbies,

but Jon didn't really care for the noise. I took to practicing whenever he wasn't around. He probably forgot I even play at all."

My fucking father. I loved him, I really did, but he was so damn rigid and set in his ways. You could set a watch by his daily routine. He didn't tolerate noise, messes, or feelings of any kind. The only person I'd ever seen him show any sort of affection toward was Suzanne, Hayden's mom. There wasn't anything he wouldn't do for her. The rest of us be damned.

"I'm sorry my father made you feel that way. You have a gift. You should share it."

"Yeah. Maybe." He moved on to another song, this time a sultry version of "Santa Baby." He sang with a flirty demeanor, and that, combined with the velvety timbre of his voice, had my dick stirring in my pants once again. I hadn't had any more alcohol since dinner, so with the effects of the liquor mostly worn off, it was getting harder and harder to ignore the effect he had on me. He was beautiful when he sang, like his soul was lit from the inside out, and like a moth to a flame, I found myself drawn to his light.

Abruptly, I stood, and he stopped playing mid-song, eyes wide in confusion. This madness had to stop. I could no longer deny the attraction I felt for him, but that didn't mean I had to act on it. I *couldn't* act on it. There were rules in society. You didn't fuck around with your stepsibling. It didn't matter that we were both grown adults and hadn't been raised together. It would tear our family apart. My father, in particular, would *never* understand.

"I'm exhausted. I think I'm going to head to bed." In the sudden silence of the cabin, my voice was unnaturally loud, as if I had no control over the volume.

"Oh, okay." He laid the guitar in the case and rose to

stand, facing me, just a few feet away. If he was surprised at my abrupt announcement, he didn't let on. "I'll take the couch since you were here first."

I nodded, unsure what else to say, desperate to escape to the bedroom before he caught sight of the raging erection tenting my pants. "I'll just brush my teeth, and then I'll be out of your way."

"Yeah, okay. Sounds good."

I hurried to the bedroom to grab my dopp kit before returning to the bathroom. Hayden had moved the stool back to its spot and was now sitting on the edge of the couch, strumming his guitar softly and humming to himself.

I made quick work of my nightly routine and then stepped back into the living room. "It's all yours," I said, standing awkwardly in front of the fireplace.

He looked up from his guitar. "Okay. Thanks." His smile was full of warmth, making me feel even worse about my attraction to him. He'd likely think I was a dirty old man if he knew what had been going on in my pants most of the night.

I nodded once more and headed into the bedroom, closing the door behind me. I climbed into bed, shut off the bedside lamp, and pulled the covers up over me.

And stared at the ceiling for hours.

4

HAYDEN

December 24

It had been an absolute garbage night of sleep. My brain had bounced between the argument I'd had with Dad yesterday morning and the weird-as-fuck evening I'd had with Jonathan. Back and forth, back and forth, over and over, until I'd thrown my blanket off, and since the reception was shitty out here and I couldn't stream anything, I resigned myself to reading a book on my Kindle app. My eyes had finally begun to droop, so I'd set my phone aside and fallen asleep.

I had no idea how long I slept before being woken up by Jonathan stumbling through the cabin in the dark, but however long it had been, it hadn't been nearly long enough. He knocked into something and muttered a whispered curse before finally making it into the bathroom. Shortly thereafter, I heard the sound of the shower running. I had no idea what time it was because I'd forgotten to plug my phone in, but it was still dark, which, to my mind, made it entirely too early to be taking a shower.

The steady sound of water falling in the shower had nearly put me back to sleep when a very distinct groan caught my attention, causing my eyes to spring open and putting my ears on full alert. A grunt and another groan, this one louder than the last, had my cock taking notice too. Surely he wasn't... Not with me in the next room and only a thin door separating us.

Too late, though, because I was already imagining it. Jonathan in the shower, cock in hand, stroking steadily up and down. Was he thick or long? Or both? He was probably using his left hand since his right was bandaged. Would that make it sloppy and frustrating? Or would changing it up make it more interesting?

Curiosity overriding good sense, I lowered the waistband of my joggers, my cock springing free, bouncing against my bare belly. I licked my palm and took my shaft in my left hand, stifling my own groan as pleasure coursed through me. I moved my other hand lower, rolling one ball and then the other, as I continued stroking, picking up the pace. Did Jonathan like his balls played with? Would he roll them around like I did, or would he prefer it a little rougher? I was willing to bet he liked it rough. Uptight guys like him always had a hidden freaky side.

It had been a long time since I'd imagined Jonathan this way—not since my teens. He'd held a prime spot in my spank bank roster until I'd finally outgrown my childish crush sometime during my senior year of high school. It turned out that having all of your perfect stepbrother's achievements shoved in your face at every turn while simultaneously failing everything you tried was a bit of a turn-off.

None of that was stopping me from imagining it now though.

The angle of my stroke was different using my left hand,

but that didn't diminish my pleasure. I liked to mix things up in the bedroom, so why not jack off with the opposite hand? I picked up the pace, imagining Jonathan was doing the same, my hand shuttling up and down, faster and faster. The fire had died down to embers during the night, but that didn't stop beads of sweat from forming on my brow as I worked myself over. My balls were tight and my body strained with the need to release, but it was the long, guttural moan coming from the bathroom that had my back arching and cum jetting all over my chest. Three spurts—no, four—all the way up to my shoulder, covering my abs and chest as I gritted my teeth, trying not to make a sound.

I lay there for a moment, my hand still wrapped around my spent dick, as I tried to catch my breath. I had sex regularly. I was a fan of having a good time, so why wouldn't I seek out partners who wanted the same thing? Occasionally, I was exclusive with someone, but even then, it wasn't really serious. It was always about pleasure and release and usually only lasted a few weeks. But tonight—this morning? I couldn't remember the last time I'd come so hard or for so long. Especially using my hand. No, not just my hand, my *left* hand. And the fact that it had been Jonathan I'd been thinking about while I'd done it was a fucking head trip.

The shower stopped, the sudden silence spurring me into motion. I grabbed the T-shirt I'd stripped out of last night off the floor and used it to wipe up my mess. I tucked myself away, debating what to do next. Should I act like I was still asleep? Fuck it. If he was going to jerk off in the shower right next to where I was sleeping, then he could deal with the consequences. I wasn't embarrassed. If he was, that was on him.

I leaned over and flipped on the lamp on the side table next to the couch just as Jonathan exited the bathroom, a cloud of steam billowing behind him. My cock tried to rally at the sight of his bare chest, the small patch of dark hair nestled between his pecs glistening with moisture. I watched as a droplet broke free and trailed down his abdomen before disappearing into the patch of hair peeking out of the towel he held clutched around his hips. I knew he ran regularly, had heard my mom talk about him running a couple of marathons, but I had never appreciated a lean runner's physique more than in that moment.

I returned my gaze to his face only to catch him admiring my bare chest just as openly as I'd admired his. One side of my mouth rose in a smirk as he bit the corner of his lip. I'd thought Jonathan was straight. Rebecca was the only person I'd ever heard of or known him to be with, though I assumed there had been others before her I hadn't known about. But if the way he was looking at me was any indication, he was definitely somewhere on the queer spectrum.

I rubbed my hand up and down my chest a couple of times, his eyes tracking the motion. "Like what you see?"

His eyes snapped to mine, tension filling his body. He opened and closed his mouth a couple of times, looking like a fish. Then, without a word, he turned and bolted for the bedroom.

I probably shouldn't have fucked with Jonathan like that this morning. The guy was clearly going through some shit, but I just couldn't help but mess with him a little. He was always so perfect. So polished and put together. Catching him looking at me like that, with lust in his eyes, even after what had obviously been a jack-off session in the shower, was too much of a temptation. Besides, maybe he could do with a little distraction. I sure as shit could use one.

After taking a quick shower, I started a pot of coffee and whipped up a couple of omelets, which I was just plating when Jonathan reemerged from the bedroom. I was fairly certain he was free-balling it in the gray sweats he wore. They were snug enough that I could see his dick print. His chest was no longer bare, though he wore a simple long-sleeved fitted tee that hugged the toned chest I'd gotten a view of this morning. His short brown hair was perfectly styled, of course, but he hadn't shaved, and I liked the bit of scruff I could see around his jawline. I'd never seen him so casual.

I set the plates on either side of the table, then joined him at the window, handing him a mug of black coffee. He avoided my gaze as he accepted the mug but said, "Thank you," after taking a sip.

We stood a moment, staring out at the dazzling beauty of the sparkling white landscape. It was a winter wonderland. Tree branches hung heavy under the burden of so much snow, and some of the smaller plants were nothing more than lumps of white.

"Looks like we're not going anywhere anytime soon," I murmured, breaking the silence.

He sighed as if the thought of being trapped here with me was too awful to contemplate. "I suppose you're right."

"You weren't planning on going anywhere for a while anyway, right?" Judging by the amount of food he'd stocked, I had assumed he was planning to be here for at least a week.

"Yeah, but that was before..."

"Before I showed up," I finished for him. It stung

knowing my presence here was so offensive to Jonathan, but I plastered on a bright smile and pulled out my chair. "Well, we might as well make the best of it. We should eat before it gets cold."

He sat but didn't pick up his fork. "I didn't mean anything by it."

I waved him off. "It's fine. You probably just wanted some time alone after whatever happened with Rebecca. I get it. As soon as we can dig out my car, I'll be out of your hair."

"Hayden, you don't have to be in a rush to leave. It's fine." But his voice didn't sound fine. He sounded tense. Strained. It was one thing to tease him a little this morning and ruffle his feathers, but I didn't want to be a source of stress for him. I hated that I always seemed to have that effect on people.

"It's no biggie. I'm scheduled at Olive & Vine on the twenty-seventh anyway. You can handle me for three more days, right?" I flashed him a teasing smile before scooping up some eggs, trying to lighten the mood.

"Yeah, sure." He finally took a bite of his eggs and groaned in pleasure. The sound of it brought back flashes of memory from this morning, and my dick went from zero to "put me in, coach" in record time. Thankfully, the table hid the evidence.

I took a few more bites, surreptitiously pushing down my cock with my other hand under the table, willing myself to calm the fuck down. He clearly didn't want me here and was only tolerating my presence because he was polite. I was sure the last thing he wanted was me hitting on him. In fact, the more I thought about it, I was sure I'd imagined that look of lust in his eyes this morning. I was probably just projecting my horniness on him.

We ate in silence, and just like last night, I was at a loss for topics of conversation. Jonathan seemed to have that effect on me. Most of the time, I was a Chatty Cathy, my brain churning out words without a filter in a rambling stream-of-consciousness. But with Jonathan, I second-guessed everything I wanted to say, convinced he'd think it was dumb.

Fortunately, it was a lighter meal, so the awkwardness didn't continue for too long before we were both finished. We took the plates to the kitchen, where I cleaned up—Jonathan didn't fight me on washing the dishes this time—and then retired to the living area with fresh mugs of coffee in hand. I could say one thing for him: he hadn't skimped on the good coffee.

He took the couch, and wanting to give him space, I grabbed my phone off the charger and sat on the lumpy recliner. Wi-Fi was unavailable and cell service was spotty in our remote location, so streaming was out of the question. I tried scrolling my socials, but just as I'd discovered in the middle of the night, I could get a couple of posts to load but couldn't respond, and as soon as I tried to scroll, I got the spinning wheel of doom that told me new posts weren't incoming any time soon.

I pulled up my Kindle app and tried to get back into the book I'd been reading in the wee hours, but I couldn't focus. Reading was like that for me. My brain was either completely engrossed, laser-focused for hours, sometimes reading an entire book in one sitting, or I was like a squirrel hopped up on Pixy Stix, my eyes darting from line to line without any of it actually sinking in.

When I caught myself reading the same sentence for the fifth time, I gave up, dropping my phone in my lap and looking over to see what Jonathan was doing. I had one foot tucked under me and the other on the ground, gently pushing myself from side to side now that I'd discovered this recliner could swivel. His eyes flicked over to me, probably distracted by my inability to sit still, and he let out a sigh. He sounded annoyed. Again.

"Sorry. I'm just bored. What do you usually do when you come up here?"

"I read." He looked pointedly at the Kindle he was holding.

"Is that all you were going to do for days and days? How long were you planning on being up here, anyway?"

With another sigh, he closed the cover on his Kindle and set it aside. "I did plan to do a lot of reading while I was up here. But sometimes I also watch old movies." He nodded toward the stack of DVDs sitting under the TV mounted on brackets in the corner. "Or when the weather's favorable, I go for a hike. What did you think you were going to do once you got up here?"

"I...didn't really think that far ahead."

"That tracks," he said with a roll of his eyes.

"Hey. Don't be a dick." He wasn't totally wrong. Not thinking ahead was one of the hallmarks of my personality. But I was getting tired of him pointing out all my flaws. I beat myself up enough, thank you.

He looked at least a little contrite, though he didn't offer an apology. I thought about putting in a movie, but I was struck with an idea.

"Wanna play Truth or Dare?"

5

JONATHAN

"Truth or Dare? What are we? Twelve?" I just wanted to read my book. Read and put the sight of him sprawled out on the couch this morning, toned chest on display, out of my mind. I didn't want to think about his built-by-pilates body at all. Or how hard I'd come in the shower this morning after tossing and turning for hours before finally giving in and jacking off to thoughts of him. I just wanted all of that to go away. I didn't need these intrusive thoughts and the havoc they had the potential to wreak on my life. I'd had enough upheaval in the last year, and I'd be damn sure I didn't bring any more of that shit with me into the new year.

It was Hayden's turn to roll his eyes. "Didn't you ever play in college?"

"Absolutely not." Total lie. I'd been in a fraternity. We did all sorts of dumb shit like that, but Hayden didn't need to know that. Some experiences were best left in distant memory. Or better yet, forgotten entirely.

"Come oooonnn..." He bounced up and down,

30

stretching out the word like a toddler begging for a piece of candy despite being told no.

God, he could be so annoying. "Fine," I bit out, knowing he was only going to drive me crazier if I didn't give in. "But I'm putting a time limit on this nonsense. You have one hour."

"Yes!" He leaped out of the chair, raced into the kitchen, and started pulling open cabinets.

"What are you looking for?"

"Alcohol."

"It's ten in the morning."

"Right." He finally found the cabinet that held the alcohol and pulled several bottles down, lining them up on the breakfast bar. He looked at me, brows lifted. "Pick your poison."

"I'm not drinking at ten a.m."

"Why not?"

"What do you mean, 'why not?' Did you not hear the part about it being ten in the *morning*?"

"So? It's not like we have any place to be. Let's do a little day drinking!" He waggled his eyebrows and turned to grab two glasses from the cabinet. "If you don't pick, I'm going to pick for you..."

Good lord. This kid—adult, he was a goddamned *adult* —was going to be the death of me. How had he gone from a concerned caretaker who'd shared a moment of earnest vulnerability and depth with his music last night to this...frat boy?

Exasperated, I let out a harsh sigh. "Whiskey." I'd killed the bourbon last night, but I was pretty sure we had at least one bottle of whiskey in the mix.

"Jameson or Johnny Walker Black?"

"Jameson is fine. How are we going to play this with alcohol?"

"It's just like Truth or Dare, but you have a third option to take a shot." He set the glasses in front of us, pouring a finger of whiskey in mine and a shot of vodka in his. "If you don't like the question for truth or the challenge for dare, you can take a shot instead."

Lord. I had a feeling I wasn't going to like this. Not one fucking bit.

The first couple of questions were easy softballs. I chose truth first, and Hayden asked me my middle name. Easy. I told him Lucius, which I actually kind of liked, but he immediately started calling me Lucy, so now that was something I was going to have to live with for the rest of my life. I asked him the same question, but his middle name was Alan, so nothing too interesting there.

We continued at an easy pace, feeling each other out, neither wanting to ask anything too challenging for fear of retaliation. It was like a very sedate game of chicken. In the fourth round, Hayden chose dare, and it took me forever to come up with something that wasn't wildly inappropriate. I was not the creative sort, but I didn't think challenging my stepbrother to jerk off in front of me was the best move. I finally challenged him to stand outside in the snow in his underwear for three minutes.

Terrible idea.

I'd intended it to be more about him standing out in the cold and freezing his nuts off, but when he flashed a wide grin, then stood and performed a strip tease, I realized I'd grossly miscalculated. He pulled up his crew neck slowly, revealing each individual ab muscle, one by one. The light had been dim when I'd caught sight of him this morning, but now, in full daylight, with the sun streaming in through the windows, I could see every perfectly defined muscle in his torso. I swallowed hard as he pulled the shirt over his head, shaking his hair and winking at me—fucking *winking* —before turning around. I openly gaped at the sight of his strong back but damn near swallowed my tongue when he slowly lowered his joggers, revealing a perfectly rounded ass, clad only in tight navy briefs adorned with snowflakes. The sight of those snowflakes should have been ridiculous, but I was so lost in the beauty of *him* that I barely noticed. He dropped the pants to the floor, then stepped out of them, turning back around to face me. He stood wide, hands held out in a 'what do you think?' gesture, his erection proudly on display.

Good god. He was hard. If not at full mast, at least halfway there. Was this turning him on? It was one thing for me to be attracted to him. I could keep it locked down. It was quite another if it was reciprocated. I'd already seen how relentless he could be when he latched on to something. I'd just have to make sure he never *ever* knew how he affected me.

I schooled my features, doing my best to revert to the same impassive expression I wore most of the time. "Your time doesn't start until you get outside."

He turned and strode—no, *sauntered,* cocky as fuck— toward the door. He pulled it open, letting in a gust of cold air that did nothing to dissipate the heat Hayden had stirred in me with his little strip tease. He waggled his eyebrows *again,* then stepped outside.

I barely had the presence of mind to start the timer, and then I downed my whiskey, hoping it would settle my frayed nerves. I poured a generous two fingers and drained my glass again. Hayden had a way of getting under my skin and turning everything on its head. I *hated* that feeling. Hated feeling out of control. I liked my life to be orderly and predictable, and Hayden was the exact opposite.

Last night, he'd taken me completely by surprise with the way he'd tenderly bandaged my hand and then cooked dinner. I hadn't bought ingredients for fancy meals, thinking it would just be me out here at the cabin, but Hayden had still managed to make a decent meal without burning anything down. Then he'd gotten out his guitar, and my world tilted again. That smooth, sultry voice. The vulnerability in the way he'd played. I'd begun to see him in a new light.

This morning, he'd turned into something else again. The antsy, restless Hayden had been more what I was used to. But this sexy, flirty side...it left my head spinning and my cock hard.

My timer went off, and I crossed to the door to let Hayden back in. I opened it and turned without a word, leaving him to follow. The door slammed shut and he shoved past me, launching himself onto the couch and pulling the old afghan off the back to cover himself. He sat in a ball with the blanket wrapped around him, only his face poking out.

It was at that point I realized I was three sheets to the wind. Or maybe not quite. Two sheets then. One and a half. Final answer. I was one and a half sheets to the wind.

Teeth chattering, he said, "Truth or Dare?"

Concerned with how he might retaliate with a dare, I chose truth.

He made a production of thinking as if he was trying to

decide which question would torture me the most. Finally, he asked, "Are you bisexual?"

What the fuck? I hadn't seen that coming. I'd been more prepared for questions about Rebecca and the divorce. "Yes."

"That's it? Just 'yes?'"

"What do you want me to say? It's not something I've ever tried to hide."

"Do Mom and Jon know?" he pressed.

"Of course."

"Well, *I* didn't know." His pout was adorable. No, *not* adorable. Annoying. Mostly.

I shrugged. "I came out in high school, long before you and I ever met."

"I never saw you with a guy before Rebecca."

"Did you see me with anyone before Rebecca?" I challenged.

He thought for a moment. "I guess not."

"Rebecca's the only person I've ever brought home. I prefer to keep my personal life private."

"Even with your dad?"

"Especially with my father, yes." My father was a hard man to please. He had strong opinions on nearly everything. I'd learned a long time ago that it was easier to hold my cards close to the vest rather than risk his judgment.

"Why with your father in particular?"

So. Many. Questions.

"I think it's your turn." I turned it on him. "Truth or Dare?"

"Aw, come on, Lucy!" Again, with the pout. He was killing me with that face.

I merely raised one eyebrow.

"Fine. After that last dare, I'm going with truth."

"Alright." I thought for a moment, though the whiskey was softening the edges a bit and making it a little harder to focus. "You didn't answer my question last night. What kind of career do you really want?"

"I don't recall that question."

"Well, I don't believe I phrased it exactly that way, but I asked about turning one of your hobbies into a career, and you changed the subject."

"Maybe there's a reason for that." The playful light was gone from his eyes. Sober me would have probably let it go, but whiskey-infused me had to know.

"Listen, you chose the game. You chose truth."

"Pass me my glass." He poked just his hand out of the blanket, waiting for me to hand it to him.

"You're not going to answer the question?"

"No, I'll answer it, but I'm going to have a goddamn shot first."

I picked up his glass and handed it to him. He downed the shot and held it back out. "More."

"Seriously? Is it really that bad?" I obliged him and poured a little more of the clear liquid into the glass.

"It's not bad. It's just...I've never told anyone before."

"No one?"

He shook his head and then tossed back the liquid I'd poured.

He straightened in his seat, still looking ridiculous the way he was wrapped up in his blanket, with just his head and hand visible, yet he seemed resolved. "I want to be a musician."

6

HAYDEN

Jonathan stared at me in silence, and as the seconds ticked by, I wilted. I could actually feel it, my body curling in on itself as if I could make my six-foot frame as small as possible.

Without looking at him, I held out my glass once again. When I didn't hear any liquid being poured out, I looked back at him. He looked shocked. Wow. Was it really so hard to believe? Had I completely misread his reaction to my music last night? He'd said I was amazing and had a gift. Was he just being polite?

"Listen, if you're not going to say anything, at least trade me the glass for the bottle."

That seemed to get his attention, and he sprang into action, taking the glass from my hand and replacing it with the bottle as requested. I immediately placed it to my lips, fire burning my throat as I swallowed. I was probably going to regret that later, but fuck it.

"I'm sorry. I just wasn't expecting you to say that."

"Thanks, man. Appreciate the support." I stood, shedding the blanket and setting the bottle on the coffee table so I could reach for my pants.

I pulled my clothes on much quicker than I'd taken them off. That had been a game. I'd wanted to see what he'd do. See if I could ruffle those perfectly groomed feathers of his again. Now, I just wanted to make a hasty exit.

"Game's over," I said, snatching up the bottle and retreating toward the bedroom. I'd just lock myself in there for the next twenty or thirty years. It'd be fine.

Before I could make it through the door, Jonathan grabbed my arm, halting my escape.

"Wait." I let out a huff but didn't look at him. "I'm sorry. We don't have to play the game, but please come back and sit down."

I chanced a look at him. His blue eyes were full of concern, and for a moment, I forgot why we were standing there. I was transfixed. What I'd felt for him all those years ago had been a silly childhood crush fueled by teenage hormones, but this was something else. Something more... adult. I'd never, not in a million years, ever thought he'd look at me like that. With anything other than...I don't know. Annoyance. Indifference. Tolerance. I didn't trust my read of him in that moment. I was too vulnerable to believe it.

When I didn't respond, he slid his hand down my arm, linking his fingers with mine and giving a little tug. "Please? Please come sit back down." My eyes traveled the same path his hand had, down my arm to where our fingers were now loosely threaded. I marveled at the sight of it. The way his fingers—a little more slender than mine, his skin a little lighter too—looked just right together.

Was he drunk? I didn't think he'd had any alcohol, but maybe he'd had some when I was outside. I couldn't make sense of this behavior. The softness in his demeanor and the concerned, almost pleading look he was giving me. Alcohol seemed like the only explanation for the one-eighty he'd turned.

Hesitantly, I nodded, and he let out a sigh of relief before he turned and crossed back to the living area, not letting go of my hand, even as we sat on the couch, closer than we had been before.

"You have an amazing gift. I'm sorry I didn't say anything right away. I was just thinking how perfect it was for you. I could actually picture it."

"Are you drunk?"

"Why do you ask that?" He seemed offended, though his eyes shifted like he was avoiding my gaze.

"The Jonathan I know would give me a lecture about responsibility and how music doesn't produce a reliable income. He'd encourage me to pursue... I don't know, investment banking or something."

He finally released my hand, turning to pour alcohol into our glasses. I missed the feel of him immediately. He handed me my glass before taking his, and we both took a sip.

"Is that what your father said?"

"My father doesn't know about the music thing, but essentially, yes. He thinks I need to get a real job that actually uses my degree rather than waste my time as a server." I sipped again. "And you didn't answer my question."

"I might, perhaps, possibly be a little tipsy." He waved his hand haphazardly in front of him in what I thought was supposed to be a dismissive gesture but instead looked like he was swatting at a fly. "That's neither here nor there. What's important is that... Wait a minute. You have a degree?"

"For fuck's sake, Lucy. How many ways can you insult me

today?" I set the glass heavily on the coffee table and got up to pace the room. I was agitated. It stung, and frankly, it was really starting to piss me off. People had doubted me my whole life, but fuck if it didn't hurt to hear him say shit like that.

"Goddammit. I'm sorry. Again. I don't know why I keep saying shit like that. You're just...not what I expected."

"Well, fuck you very much. Maybe if you spent a little less time passing judgment and making assumptions about who I am, you'd stop eating your own goddamn foot."

He stood, approaching me carefully, and I stopped my pacing and faced him.

"I'm sorry."

"Yeah, you said that." I crossed my arms. I knew I was being belligerent and maybe a little childish, but I was hurt, dammit.

He took a step closer. "I mean it. I've always been an ass. I get it from my father."

"No shit." He looked nothing like his father, but in terms of personality, he was a fucking carbon copy of the man.

"I deserve that," he said as he took a step closer and placed his hand on my arm. The heat of it burned all the way through the fabric of my crewneck, and I hated the subtle way I leaned into it. My body was a traitor. "Tell me who you are."

"What?"

"You said I was making assumptions about who you are, and you're right. So, tell me. Who are you, Hayden?"

The sincerity of the question completely disarmed me. But when the hand on my arm moved to cup my cheek, my mind went completely blank. We were standing in the middle of the living room, and I didn't remember when I'd uncrossed my arms, but his chest was practically touching mine and his lips were just inches away.

I couldn't figure out how we'd gotten to this point. The last twenty-four hours had been a rollercoaster of highs and lows between the two of us. We'd both made assumptions about each other, and we'd both been wrong. But if the way he was looking at me right now was any indication, with his thumb rubbing gently back and forth over my cheek, I didn't think I was the only one feeling the attraction between us.

Maybe it was the vodka, or maybe it was the remnants of a childhood crush I'd thought I'd suppressed. Or maybe it was the sweet way he'd asked me who I was like he actually wanted to know the answer. Whatever the reason, I leaned forward and brushed his lips with mine. Once. Twice. And then I pulled back, licking my own lips to capture the whiskey-flavored taste of him.

I waited to see what his reaction would be. His expression was unreadable, but then the hand resting on my cheek slid around to the nape of my neck and he pulled me back in, pressing his lips to mine once more. He kissed me leisurely but with all the authority of a man who knew what he was doing. Lips slanted against mine, he applied more pressure, then stroked my mouth with his tongue.

I let him in. Of course, I let him in, swallowing his taste. A moan escaped me as I stepped into him, my leg sliding between his so we were aligned from chest to groin. I hissed as his erection brushed against mine, electricity rocketing through my body. Desperate for more, I threaded one hand around the nape of his neck, mirroring the hold he had on me, and squeezed his waist with the other. There wasn't a bit of fat to be found on his lean runner's body, and I kneaded the muscle there in time with the strokes of our tongues.

He growled as he bit my lip, then dove into the kiss again, this time with more intensity. I gripped the back of his head, wishing his neatly trimmed hair was just a little longer so I could yank it. Instead, I opted to trail my other hand from his waist, slipping it under the waistband of his joggers and down to his ass, grabbing a handful and holding him to me.

I had been right. He *was* free-balling. That knowledge stoked the flames of the fire raging inside me, and without breaking the kiss, I yanked his pants down to his thighs and wrapped my hand around his erection. He hissed in response and pulled away from the kiss to look at me.

"Are you sure?"

I stroked him in slow but firm strokes, watching as a battle waged in his eyes. "Are you?"

He rested his forehead against mine, taking a moment to catch his breath. I continued stroking. If he asked me to stop, I would, but I hoped he wouldn't.

He must have come to some sort of decision because before I knew what was happening, he tugged my joggers and briefs down in one fluid motion and his left hand wrapped around my cock, attempting to pace me stroke for stroke.

My knees nearly gave out, and I whimpered at the feel of his smooth hand sliding up and down my length, but he was awkward with his non-dominant hand. I swatted it away, taking both of us in my fist, and as the need to release coursed through me, I picked up the pace, dropping my head to his chest so I could watch.

The sight and feel of the two of us rubbing against each other as I stroked us in a feverish rhythm was my undoing. My orgasm barreled through me without warning, cum erupting from my tip and dripping down my hand like an ice cream cone melting in the heat of July. He squeezed my hips tightly as his orgasm followed, both of us grunting through our pleasure until I'd milked us dry.

"So that happened," I said, my sweaty forehead still resting on his chest as we both struggled to catch our breath.

He relaxed his grip on my waist, though he didn't release me right away. His softening dick slipped from my grip, and at last, he pulled away. I was scared to look at him, afraid I'd see regret lining his features, and I didn't think I could take that.

My clothes were a mess and so was the floor. I stepped all the way out of my pants and briefs, using my joggers to wipe my hands and then the floor. I stood, still avoiding his gaze, trying to decide the quickest way to make my exit, when Jonathan stopped me, once again, with a hand gently caressing my jaw.

He lifted my chin, forcing me to meet his gaze. There was a tenderness there I hadn't been expecting.

"What am I going to do with you, Hayden?"

7

———

JONATHAN

"What do you *want* to do with me?" Something was swirling in those dark eyes of his. Some unnamed emotion I couldn't identify. I thought I should be sorry for what had happened. I should regret it, should be worried about the ramifications of what we had done. But I just couldn't find it in myself to feel anything other than... Well, I wasn't sure exactly what I was feeling, but I knew it wasn't regret.

"I don't know," I answered honestly. The hazy fog of alcohol had mostly lifted, yet my thoughts wouldn't coalesce with any sort of clarity. Not with him standing so close to me. Not with both of our dicks still out. Perhaps we needed to take a moment to regroup. Yes, that was logical. Smart.

Regretfully, I took a step back, releasing him. It was harder to do than it had any right to be. "Why don't we get cleaned up? You can go first, and I'll scrounge up some lunch."

"What about your hand?"

He really was so sweet. I couldn't ever remember a time in my life when anyone had shown such concern for me. I gave him a small smile. "I think I can manage some sandwiches."

"Yeah, okay." He turned and walked toward the bathroom, grabbing his duffel on the way. The sight of him walking away from me in nothing but his crewneck, with his bare ass exposed, nearly had me calling him back for another round. But I forced myself to turn away, heading into the bedroom to change.

Hayden had taken the brunt of our mess, so cleanup was rather quick for me. I slipped on a pair of boxers and another pair of joggers and returned to the kitchen, where I opened the fridge and began pulling out the fixings for sandwiches. Unsure what he liked, I opted to leave everything out on the counter so he could assemble his own to his preference.

With the sound of the shower running as my soundtrack, I sorted through various toppings and condiments and allowed my mind to wander back over the events of the last twenty-ish hours.

Since he'd arrived last night, I'd gotten drunk twice—though, to be fair, I was already drunk when he arrived—jacked off twice—again, to be fair, it had been him jacking me the second time—listened to him sing, confessed my middle name, watched him perform a striptease, discussed my sexuality and his career aspirations, and stuck my foot in my mouth more than once while making an array of incorrect assumptions about him.

It was...a lot.

He was right though. I really was just like my father. Maybe not in the lusting-after-his-step-siblings department, but definitely in the passing-judgments-and-making-assumptions-while-maintaining-the-holiest-of-holier-than-thou-attitudes department.

Huh. Maybe I was still a little tipsy. Or maybe Hayden had short-circuited the part of my brain that used to think in properly constructed sentences.

But was that really who I wanted to be? Rebecca had called me anal, boring, and predictable. She'd also been exactly the same type of judgmental person I was. It was why I'd thought we were such a good match. Not because she was judgmental but because she valued the same things I did. She was punctual. Organized. She ate healthy and worked out regularly. She was career-driven and understood the value of cultivating business relationships and presenting a polished, put-together appearance. All things that were important to me as well.

But where had that left us? We'd spent the last three years focused on those things, on what I thought were things we both wanted, when in actuality, she'd been banging Jeff from marketing. Nights spent working late and dinner engagements that'd been rescheduled hadn't been related at all to a drive to further her career. As inconvenient as those things had been, I'd admired her sense of drive and ambition. I had those things too. Instead, nights working late had been spent at happy hour getting tipsy, and dinner engagements had been canceled so she could fuck Jeff at his condo across town.

Boring. Anal. Predictable.

Apparently, the fact I was boring sent her looking for fun with someone else. And the fact that I was predictable made it easy for her to know what time I'd be home so she could sneak around behind my back.

It was all bullshit, of course. Maybe I was boring and predictable, but that didn't excuse her cheating on me. What it did do was cause me to reevaluate some things. The fact that Rebecca had upended my life, my carefully constructed routine, was more upsetting than her absence from it. It wasn't so much that I hadn't loved her as that I didn't really know if I was capable of loving anyone. She'd been beautiful, of course, and we'd been compatible in the bedroom. But fuck...was *compatible* ever a word you wanted to use to describe your relationship with someone you were sleeping with? That you were *married* to?

I'd settled for *compatible* because it hadn't really occurred to me that there could be more. Love, the kind with soulful looks and passionate embraces, was the stuff of movies and romance novels. Sure, I could recognize that my father loved Suzanne. And she was a lovely woman. But to my mind, they were the exception, not the norm.

Hayden emerged from the shower, interrupting my melancholy reflection. I looked up as he walked out, all thoughts of Rebecca vanishing as I took a moment to really look at him. His hair was damp and a little haphazard as if he hadn't done more than run his fingers through it. He had changed into another pair of joggers, this time gray, and a faded black long-sleeved tee that clung to every muscle in his torso. He was fucking beautiful.

He caught my eye, caught me ogling him, and that playfulness was back. He shot me a wink before slowly making his way across the living room to the kitchen, where I was still standing at the counter. I felt my lips curve into a smile, almost as if my mouth had a mind of its own. He had this way about him that annoyed the shit out of me but still somehow had me smiling, whether I liked it or not.

I nudged a plate toward him. "I started to make you a sandwich, but I realized I didn't know what you liked."

"I see how it is," he teased playfully, "I make you an actual meal, and you can't even complete the task of making a simple sandwich."

"Fuck off," I said without any real heat. "I was trying to be considerate of your tastes."

"Sure. Keep telling yourself that." He bro-slapped my back, and I rolled my eyes.

We ate at the counter while standing, not bothering to make our way over to the table. I filled a couple of glasses with water and set one in front of him.

He raised his eyebrows at me as if to say, *really?*

"I figured we should probably hydrate after the drinking this morning."

"Thanks, *Dad.*"

I cringed. "No. No, thank you. Absolutely not. You are not calling me that. It's weird enough we're stepbrothers."

"So? Who cares?"

I was sure the look on my face was incredulous. "You're kidding me. Our parents? Other people?" How could he be so blasé about this?

"Oh, well, if other people care, that completely changes things."

I knew he was poking fun, but I was legitimately concerned about this. "Don't be a dick. Pretty sure banging your stepbrother is frowned upon by pretty much everyone."

"So we're gonna bang?" He smiled as he took a huge bite of his sandwich, chewing obnoxiously. He was having a good time with this.

"I haven't ruled it out," I said evenly, wanting to turn the tables on him. Lust flashed in his eyes. He swallowed his bite and straightened from the counter, stalking toward me.

Oh shit.

"Watch out there, Lucy. You're playing with fire." He got up in my space, and it wasn't until my ass hit the edge of the counter that I realized he'd backed me into it. He'd cornered me. I was used to being in charge in nearly every aspect of my life, but for the first time, I found myself wanting to give up control. Still, I had to make sure he was thinking this through. One of us needed to be rational here.

"It seriously doesn't bother you that we're stepbrothers? You don't worry about what our parents will think?"

He shrugged. "Honestly, it's none of their business. Do you plan on telling them?" He leaned in and nipped at my neck just above the collar of my shirt. "We're not talking about a marriage commitment here. We're trapped in a cabin in a blizzard, and obviously, there's some attraction between us. Why not fuck around?"

"You want this? Me?"

He nipped at my ear, his breath tickling the fine hairs of my neck. "Would I be doing this if I didn't?" Goosebumps broke out all over my skin as he licked a stripe from my ear to the neckline of my shirt. He pulled it aside, exposing my collarbone. He licked and sucked the hollow of my shoulder until I was sure I'd have a hickey there, but it felt so damn good.

Sex with Rebecca had been about *her*. And that fact hadn't ever really bothered me. Getting her off was always the end goal. I got an orgasm in the end, so what did I care if it was more about her than me? The destination was the most important part, regardless of the path we took to get there.

As his lips trailed across the base of my throat, nipping and licking a path from one shoulder to the other, I realized I'd never fully understood just how good it could feel to spend a little more time on the journey before arrival.

His hand found its way around to my backside, and he pulled me into him, grinding our cocks together through way too many layers of fabric. Still, the feel of his dick against mine was a reminder of just who I was doing this with. And damned if my mouth didn't shoot off one more time. "It really doesn't bother you?"

Abruptly, he pulled away. "Clearly, it bothers *you*. Do I need to stop?"

I shrugged. "No. Yes. I don't know." *Fuck.* I always had an answer. Always. This was so fucking confusing.

"Anything other than a yes is still a no. I'm not going to take this any further if you're not sure what you want." He walked back over to his sandwich and took another bite, casual as could be. Meanwhile, my cock was trying to punch a hole through my joggers, my pulse was still racing, and I had whiplash from the abrupt change of course. And I had no one to blame but myself and my big mouth.

"Look, I guess I'm having a hard time wrapping my head around this."

He set his sandwich down and looked at me, crossing his arms and resting his hip against the counter. I couldn't help but allow my eyes to dart down to his crotch, noting he was having just as much of a problem in the pants department as I was, despite his casual attitude. If he noticed me look-ing, he didn't mention it.

He swallowed his bite and let out a breath. "So here's the deal. Yes, we're stepbrothers, but it's not like we grew up together, right? And how many times have we actually seen each other in the last eight years since our parents got married? Two or three times a year?"

I shrugged again. "Yeah, I guess that's about right."

"We barely know each other. We're not blood-related. We're both single, trapped by a million inches of snow with nothing else to do, and I don't know about you, but I'm horny as fuck. I think you're overthinking it."

I wasn't sure if I was thinking with my head or my dick,

but what he was saying was making some sense. "If we do this, it's just until you go home. Suzanne and my father never need to know."

Something crossed over his features so quickly that I thought I imagined it. "Fine by me. I'm not really a commitment guy."

"Alright."

"Alright, like 'let's get it on?'"

I rolled my eyes. "Yeah, Hayden. Let's do it."

8

―――――――

HAYDEN

That was all the green light I needed. Without another word, I dropped to my knees in front of Jonathan. His breath caught as I looked up at him, then focused my attention on the bulge right in front of me.

Slowly, I lowered the waistband of his joggers, torn between watching his face and eyeing his cock as I exposed it one excruciating inch at a time. It was fucking beautiful. Long and thick with a vein running down the underside. I couldn't wait to feel it on my tongue.

I leaned in, nuzzling his crotch and inhaling the musky scent of him before licking a stripe right along that vein and taking him all the way to the back of my throat in one fluid motion. His hand gripped my hair fiercely as he fought to control himself. Jonathan's tense body was like a live wire ready to spark. I slid up and down slowly, taking my time to make sure he felt my mouth, wet and slippery, on every inch of his dick.

"Lucy, look at me." I waited until his lust-hazed eyes cleared enough to focus on me. "Relax." I squeezed his tight ass and ran my hand down the backs of his thighs, his hamstrings stretched taught with tension.

He reached down and ran his fingers through my hair, combing them through the mostly-dry strands. "Don't want to come yet."

"You just came an hour ago. Aren't old guys like you supposed to have a longer refractory period?" I flashed him a cheeky smile.

"First of all, fuck off." He tugged at my hair just hard enough to make his point. "Second, it's been a...while since I've had a blowjob." The shy look on his usually arrogant face was disarming. "It feels good," he said softly.

"Rebecca didn't...?" I raised my eyebrows in question.

He slowly shook his head from side to side, his fingers continuing to run through my hair almost absent-mindedly.

I stood abruptly, taking his hand in mine and pulling him toward the bedroom. "Come on," I said unnecessarily. It was pretty obvious where we were headed in the tiny cabin.

"Why?"

"Because we're doing this right," I said, without turning back to look at him, continuing to tug him in the direction I wanted to go. "I want to take my time with you, and we need a bed for that."

He came to an abrupt halt, tugging my hand to stop my forward progress. I turned and looked at him. "What's wrong?"

"We need to brush our teeth."

"What?"

"We just ate lunch. We need to brush our teeth." He looked like a petulant toddler trying to explain to his father why he needed a red cup instead of blue.

"Honey, I don't need a clean mouth for what I'm planning to do to you." The smirk I gave him was full of lascivious promise.

He swallowed hard, his Adam's apple bobbing. His blue eyes darkened with lust, but he held his ground. "I want to kiss you. And I can't kiss you after eating a mouthful of roast beef and mustard."

Bless his sweet, persnickety heart. The more time I spent with him, the more his little quirks became less annoying and more endearing.

I tightened my grip on his hand again and changed direction, pulling him toward the bathroom, where we both brushed our teeth so thoroughly that even the toughest of dental hygienists would have been impressed. My cock had softened some in the interim, but not my desire. If anything, I was more determined to get him out of his head and wild with lust.

"Satisfied?" I asked, smiling so he'd know I was teasing.

He returned my smile, then leaned forward, cupped my cheek, and kissed me so sweetly, so tenderly, my heart fluttered in my chest.

Huh. That was a new feeling.

He pulled back and smiled. "Yeah. I'm satisfied." I nodded, too dazed to form words. This time, it was Jonathan who pulled me toward the bedroom.

We crossed the threshold, and I started to reach for the light, but Jonathan stopped me and crossed over to lift the shade covering the windows. I squinted as my eyes adjusted to the light streaming into the small room. It was nearly blinding as it bounced off all that white outside. Trees laden with thick layers of snow looked like they'd been frosted with glitter. It was breathtaking, but not nearly so much as the man now standing naked in front of me.

While I'd been admiring the view outside and trying to

adjust to the blinding light streaming in, Jonathan had stripped down to nothing. I was sorry I'd missed the show, but I took the time now to admire every inch of his lean runner's body. A small patch of hair was nestled between his pecs, then trailed down his abdomen to the darker patch of neatly trimmed curls at his groin. It came as no surprise that he kept himself as neatly groomed down below as he did the rest of his body. His muscled legs were covered in a light layer of hair that I couldn't wait to feel wrapped around me, but right now, my attention was focused on his pretty dick, jutting proudly from his body as if it was reaching only for me.

I stepped forward, removing my shirt as I did so, and tossed it aside without care where it landed. I stepped out of my joggers and briefs, leaving those in a pile on the floor as well. And then, finally, with one more step, I was pressed against him, with nothing between us from shoulders to toes. The bedroom was slightly cooler than the rest of the house, sending a shiver down my spine, even as a fire raged beneath my skin.

The look in his eyes said there was a fire beneath his as well.

Surprising us both, I pulled him into a hug. I'd meant to kiss him, lick him, maybe grab his dick and stroke. But suddenly, I'd found myself wanting to hold him. To feel his chest pressed to mine, our hearts racing against each other as if they could beat out a language only meant to be understood by the other.

We were of a similar height, so our chins rested comfortably on the other's shoulders as we held each other closely. My eyes burned with emotion, and so I slammed them shut, even as I breathed in his scent and savored the feel of him in my arms.

Fuck. This wasn't supposed to be about *feelings.* This was supposed to be a bit of fun while we blew off some steam. A way to pass the time while stranded in the wilderness. But fuck if I could remember the last time someone had held me.

I didn't want to let go.

And for that reason, I deliberately pulled back. "Get on the bed," I said gruffly, hoping Jonathan would mistake it for desire rather than whatever the fuck this emotion was.

"How do you want me?"

Was there a sexier question in the universe?

"On your back."

I watched as he climbed onto the bed, his lithe body moving into position as requested.

"You're so goddamn beautiful, do you know that?"

I climbed on the bed, crawling up his body until I straddled his waist, my ass resting just above his cock. The feel of his erection nestled in my crack was almost too much of a temptation to resist. I wanted nothing more than to impale myself on his beautiful dick, but we hadn't talked about topping and bottoming, and I had a feeling that conversation might scare him away.

Instead, I leaned forward and kissed him, this time claiming his mouth with every bit of lust in my body. It was dirty and raw and *needy,* and he returned it with every bit as much enthusiasm until I realized that if I didn't pull back, we were going to end up in a frotting situation that was going to end much more quickly than I wanted.

I enjoyed frotting as much as the next guy, but I wanted this to be about *him,* and I wanted to use my mouth.

He chased the kiss as I pulled away as if he didn't ever want it to end, but as I trailed my lips down the scruff of his jaw and nibbled at his ear, he arched his head back and whimpered. I groaned as I nibbled and sucked, loving his responsiveness.

I was willing to bet sex with Rebecca had been a performative act. One in which he held himself carefully in control until the moment they both came. And I was also willing to bet that even then, at the height of orgasm, he'd restrained himself to nothing more than a grunt or two.

That simply wouldn't do. I wanted to tear down his carefully built walls bit by bit until he was a screaming, writhing mess beneath me.

I wanted to wreck him.

Abandoning his ear, I continued my exploration down his body using my tongue and my teeth, occasionally pausing to suck a bit of his skin until I arrived at one dusky nipple.

He hissed as I licked a wide stripe across it with the flat of my tongue, then blew a tiny stream of air over it, and I watched as the little bud tightened until it was hard enough to cut glass. I flicked it again with my tongue before sliding over to the other side and repeating the action.

"Jesus-mother-fucking-Christ," came out of his mouth on a groan as his hips bucked up, his ass nearly leaving the mattress, as his cock desperately tried to find some friction.

"So dirty. And on Christmas Eve, no less," I teased before returning my lips to his body, following his happy trail down his abdomen to where a string of precum stretched from his dick to his belly. He was leaking like crazy.

"If you don't get on with it, I'm going to...ungh."

I took him all the way to the back of my throat, swallowing around his length, then applying suction as I slowly pulled back off him.

"What was that? You're going to do what, exactly?"

He lifted his head and glared at me. He was trying to

look menacing, and I'm sure it worked on his employees, but I merely found it adorable. He was all bark and no bite. Grinning, I decided to put him out of his misery.

I licked down his shaft again, this time continuing farther down to mouth his balls. "Up," I said and tapped his knees, signaling him to pull them back for me.

"What?" His voice held a tinge of alarm.

"Pull your knees back. Let me see that pretty hole."

His legs did quite the opposite, squeezing my shoulders where I was nestled between them. "You want to look at my asshole?" The tone of his voice and the look on his face—he was so affronted by this idea that I let out a sharp burst of laughter.

"Lucy, have you never been rimmed?"

"No, of course not. No. Never." He started to scramble away from me, but I grabbed his leg, stopping him before he could get away.

"I'm sorry I laughed, and we don't have to do that if you aren't comfortable, but believe me when I tell you, it's fucking amazing."

"Seriously? You *want* to put your mouth *there*?" His tone was incredulous.

I lifted my head, making sure he could fully see my face so he'd know I meant it when I said, "I really, really do."

"But..."

"I wouldn't do anything I didn't want. Promise."

He nodded.

"Say it. Say the words. Or we don't do it. I love sucking dick just as much, and we can just stick to that."

"No, you can go ahead. You can...rim me." I hid my smile at his choice of words, lest he get embarrassed again. We needed to have a talk later about just exactly how far he'd gone with a man and what his limits were, but for now, I had enough consent for what I had planned.

"Lift your knees." This time, he complied, hesitantly pulling them back to his chest, revealing his pretty pink hole, just begging to be stretched by my tongue.

I leaned forward and gently licked at his entrance, allowing him to adjust to the sensation. His erection had flagged a bit as he'd gotten up in his head, but I was gratified to see his dick perking up at the first couple of swipes. Emboldened by the sight, I licked again, a little more earnestly, lapping at his entrance with sloppy enthusiasm. He let loose a whimper, and I smiled. With one hand, I reached up and rolled each of his balls between my fingers as I used the other to spread his cheeks. Pointing my tongue, I pushed inside.

He jolted at the intrusion, and I paused, giving him time to tell me to stop.

"*Hayden,*" he whined. "Don't stop."

I dove back in, pushing in a little farther with each stroke, softening his entrance as his hips jerked and bucked, and he writhed under my tongue.

I felt his balls draw up tight under my fingers and knew he was close, so reluctantly, I pulled back. I wanted him to come in my mouth.

He lifted his head to look at me, irritation on his face as he'd been denied the release he so desperately wanted. "Why'd you stop?"

I flashed a shit-eating grin as I shifted so my face was hovering over his dick. I stuck out my tongue and licked his slit, savoring the salty taste of his precum like I was a cum connoisseur.

He watched me intently as I stuck my tongue out again, this time swirling it around the head before licking my way down, down, down, to the base and back up again. By the time I returned to the tip, his head had dropped back onto the pillow and his eyes were squeezed shut like he couldn't take much more. His hands, still holding his legs back, were gripping hard enough to leave bruises, and I knew I had him right where I wanted him.

Once again, I drew him all the way to the back of my throat, this time moving up and down with purpose, setting a moderate rhythm as I gauged just how much longer he'd be able to hold out. Based on the groans coming out of his mouth and the way he was bucking his hips, I figured I didn't have much time.

Moving my hand down, I tapped his hole with my index finger and paused just long enough to ask, "You gonna let me in, Lucy?"

"Yes. God yes. Just don't stop."

Smiling, I sucked on my finger before returning it to its place and pressing in slowly, allowing him to adjust. My tongue had already done some of the work to loosen him up, so my finger slipped in easily. As I continued to press in farther, I wrapped my mouth around his dick once again, this time setting a rapid pace I knew would have him shooting in moments.

Finding the spot I was looking for, I crooked my finger. Lucy's hips punched up, sending his dick into the back of my throat, nearly gagging me with the force as he exploded in my mouth.

With each pulse, I tapped that spot again and again, swallowing around him until, finally, he yanked himself out of my mouth with a curse, his overly sensitive dick softening against his thigh.

I gently removed my finger, chuckling at his reaction, trying to ignore my own aching cock's need for release. That had been hot as fuck, and would likely play out in my spank bank highlight reel for years to come, but I'd done it for him, not for myself. He'd been so tense and uptight, and I'd just wanted him to relax and let go. To have some pleasure just for pleasure's sake.

He was still breathing hard, though he'd dropped his legs and was starfished across the bed like he no longer had any control over his limbs. I climbed up his body, laying my head on his shoulder, and threw one thigh across his hip. My disgruntled dick brushed against his skin, and I hissed involuntarily.

"Wait. What about you?" he mumbled half-heartedly. I was pretty sure he had one foot across the threshold of dreamland.

"Shh. We can worry about me later."

"Okay."

Jonathan Lucius Black fell asleep, blissed out, completely naked, in broad daylight. Moments later, I fell asleep in his arms, right beside him.

9

JONATHAN

I wasn't sure how long I slept, but the light streaming through the wide-open window cast a golden hue in the room, indicating it was getting toward dusk. I couldn't remember the last time I'd taken a nap, much less one that had lasted several hours. Hayden had turned in his sleep so that he was now lying on his side with his face turned away from me, though I must have rolled over with him because his back was pressed against my chest and my arm was draped loosely over his hip. We were still lying on top of the blankets, though his body was like a furnace, keeping me warm despite the chill in the room.

My fingers traced the line of his hip absently as I thought about the things he'd done to me before we'd both passed out. In light of my reservations about our relationship to each other, I would have thought I'd be freaking out right now, but in fact, I couldn't remember the last time I'd felt so relaxed. He'd turned me inside out with the things he'd done with his tongue, things I'd never imagined I'd experience, yet he'd checked in with me at each turn, making sure I was comfortable, assuring me we'd only

62

proceed if I was ready. Then, he'd taken nothing in return. In all my life, I'd never had someone so single-mindedly focused on my wants and needs.

Warmth spread through my chest at the thought, and I suddenly found myself wanting to repay him, to make him feel just as good as he'd made me. I didn't think I was ready to try rimming him, but I'd given a few blowjobs back in college. I wasn't sure anything I did could live up to what he'd done to me, but I wanted to try.

Lifting my head, I pressed kisses along his shoulder, leisurely trailing down his arm as far as I could reach without jostling him too much. He sighed and pressed his ass back, grinding against my lengthening erection, and a groan escaped me at the contact.

"Mmm. 'S a nice way to be woken up." He turned his head back, his eyes still heavy-lidded, as he offered his mouth up to mine for a kiss.

Even half-asleep, with his hair a mess, he was beautiful. I pressed my lips to his, then said, "Lie on your back."

His lips spread in a lazy smile as he twisted to do as I asked. I'd attempted to be discreet in the way I'd admired his body this morning, but now I took my time, shamelessly taking in every inch of defined muscle and smooth skin. His complexion was just a few shades darker than mine, and had it not been winter, I imagined he'd have the type of skin that would tan nicely, whereas mine burned if I even thought about going outside.

His dick twitched, drawing my attention away from the survey of his muscles, making me wonder why I'd been looking anywhere else. He wasn't as thick as me, but he was long, with a bit of a curve, and for the first time in my life, I considered the possibility of bottoming, if only to see what that curve would do to me.

"I know my dick is a thing of beauty, but did you have me lie on my back just to admire it, or did you have something else in mind?" He had his hands tucked behind his head and was looking at me with the smirkiest of smirks. It made me want to fuck with him a little. He seemed to bring out that side in me.

"It's alright, I guess. Not as thick as mine." I shrugged and made to move back up the bed as if I was done with my examination. He put a hand on my shoulder to stop me.

"Not so fast there, Lucy. It's not the size that counts. It's how you use it." He waggled his eyebrows, and I couldn't help it. I collapsed in laughter, burying my head in his stomach.

"Your laugh is beautiful." He ran his fingers through my hair. "You should do that more often."

I looked up at him, the mirth fading and the air between us crackling with meaning. "Yeah?"

"Yeah."

Our eyes locked, some unnamed emotion passing between us. I couldn't look away. "You bring out a side of me I didn't think existed. You make me feel...lighter."

"Good. Not everything has to be serious all the time. You *are* allowed to have fun. You know that, right?"

I did know that. I just didn't know how to access that side of myself.

Somehow, Hayden had unlocked it. And it made me want more.

Unsure how to respond, I broke eye contact, returning my gaze to his cock, still standing at attention. With more confidence than I felt, I licked a stripe up the underside, just as he'd done to me, then stuck my tongue in his slit, the salty taste of him exploding on my tongue.

God, I'd forgotten how good a man could taste.

The sounds coming from Hayden were inhuman as I went to work on him in earnest. Turns out sucking dick was a lot like riding a bike, and though it'd been nearly ten years since the last time I'd given head, I hadn't forgotten how to make a man beg.

Bobbing my head up and down his length, I set a steady pace, alternating between fast and aggressive and slow and deep, with copious amounts of suction. He writhed under me, hands clenching the bedding, my hair, whatever he could get his hands on, between uttering creative streams of nonsensical curses.

"*Mother-fucking-holy-shit-goddammit-son-of-abi—ahhhh.*" Cum filled my mouth without warning, and I struggled to swallow all of it as he pumped into me in short bursts. I kept my mouth clamped around him until he finally collapsed on the bed, sated and nearly lifeless. I hadn't even had a chance to play with his balls.

I let his dick slide from my mouth, then climbed up the bed, collapsing beside him. "Damn," he finally spit out between breaths. "You're better at that than I expected."

"Hmm. I guess I'm not the only one who makes assumptions."

He chuckled and patted my thigh weakly. "Touché."

I turned on my side, propping my head in my hand to look at him. "I've had sex with men before. I'm not completely inexperienced." He turned his head on the pillow to look at me. "I just wasn't ever comfortable with ass-play."

"Your ass or someone else's ass?"

I snorted. "I've topped but never bottomed, if that's what you're asking."

"Pretty much." He turned all the way on his side, propping his head in his hand, mirroring my position. "Lucky for you, I'm vers, so I can go either way."

My dick, which had decided it still hadn't recovered enough from this afternoon's blowjob to rise to the occasion for a second round, tried valiantly to make another attempt. The refractory period really did hit different in your thirties, but perhaps with some sustenance, he could see some action later tonight.

"We never finished lunch. Maybe we should eat first. You may be in your twenties, but surely your dick still needs some recovery time?"

"Give me ten, and I'll be good to go."

"I call bullshit." I leaned forward and kissed him on his nose right as his stomach rumbled.

"Yeah, okay. Maybe we should eat."

"I t doesn't feel like Christmas Eve."

We were sitting side by side on the living room floor with our backs resting against the couch and our legs stretched out in front of us, eating frozen pizza off paper plates. "I don't know. I guess we never really did much for Christmas Eve, so it doesn't feel much different."

"Really? You didn't have any traditions with Rebecca or your dad?" He must have caught my wince because he said, "Shit. Sorry. I shouldn't have brought it up."

I snorted. "Neither of those people had a sentimental bone in their body. I think my father would have rather skipped the holidays entirely, while Rebecca was only concerned with the receiving of gifts and putting in appearances at holiday parties."

"I'm sorry. That sucks." His hand was warm where it

rested on my thigh. I was sure he meant to offer comfort, but I didn't really need it.

I shrugged my shoulders. "It's not a big deal. I'm not an overly sentimental person myself, so it never really bothered me."

Though if I were honest, that wasn't entirely true. One of the perks of my divorce was that I was no longer obligated to attend all those holiday parties, with their lukewarm food and mindless small talk. Still, there had been a time in my childhood when I'd longed for my father to make a bigger to-do about Christmas. I'd wanted to set out milk and cookies for Santa, followed by a cozy reading of *The Night Before Christmas*, just like I saw in movies. Those days were long gone now though. I hadn't even thought about any of that in years.

"Well, with Mom coming from a large Catholic family, Christmas was always a whole *thing* growing up. There was usually an entire day of baking with all the aunts and cousins the Saturday before. Then, on Christmas Eve, we would attend the children's mass at St. Anthony's, followed by chili at my Nana's. Each family would bring a crockpot of chili to share, and Nana always made her homemade cinnamon rolls to go with it. Around eleven, they'd round up all the kids to head home and go to bed so Santa could come and bring presents. When we got home, I'd put out milk and cookies for Santa and carrots for the reindeer, and then we'd read *Twas The Night Before Christmas* before bed. Even after the divorce, when he'd remarried and had my sister, my dad never fought about me being with Mom on Christmas Eve because he understood what a big deal it was."

He paused and took a bite of his pizza, oblivious to the fact that I'd suddenly found it hard to swallow past the lump in my throat. He'd just described the exact type of Christmas I'd always wanted, the dream I'd long ago buried, knowing it wasn't something my father was ever going to be capable of giving me. And as I'd gotten older, I'd convinced myself it wasn't something I'd ever really needed anyway.

But as I sat here on the floor of the cabin that had once belonged to my grandfather and listened to Hayden describe his Christmas Eve memories in picture-perfect detail, I was filled with such a deep longing for that piece of childhood that had eluded me.

And yet, watching Hayden talk about what was clearly a happy memory for him was a sight to behold. His cheeks were rosy, and his eyes were alight with pure joy as he continued to talk about his Christmas-morning traditions, which sounded like something straight out of the Hallmark channel. He was so animated with the retelling of it all that a lock of hair kept falling over his forehead, and he impatiently brushed it back over and over again, never pausing in his story.

I was so captivated by him that despite my own conflicted emotions, I leaned over and brushed that pesky strand of hair off his forehead and kissed him there, right as he was in the middle of a sentence. His words trailed off as I let my lips linger in the center of his forehead. When I pulled back, his eyes were full of questions I didn't have answers for, so I turned and gathered the paper plates, then stood and took them into the kitchen to clean up.

He followed me, of course. In the last twenty-four hours, I'd somehow gotten to know him well enough to know that my walking away wouldn't stop an onslaught of questions. But I'd needed that moment of distance anyway. I was feeling some Big Feelings, and I didn't know what to do with them or how to process them. How did people walk around feeling like this all the time? It was like having too many tabs open on your browser and not being able to find the one you were looking for.

I heard his intake of breath, and I knew a question was coming, only it wasn't a question I was expecting. "Can we watch a movie? I noticed you have *Elf* in the stack over there. We can make a new tradition."

Oddly touched that he would think of something like that and avoiding the implication that establishing a tradition implied we'd be spending Christmas together again in the future, I simply nodded my agreement.

Dinner didn't take long to clean up, nor did setting up the movie, so by the time I was finished in the kitchen, Hayden had just finished cueing it up. Without allowing myself to overthink it, I crossed to the couch and sat sideways, spreading my legs and gesturing for him to sit between them in front of me. His face lit up and he settled in, reclining his back against my chest.

It was a small couch, and we were not small guys, so it took some maneuvering, but we finally managed to find a comfortable position, and I snagged the blanket from the back of the couch to drape over us.

Unsure now what to do with my arms, I finally settled on wrapping them around his torso, and he let out a sigh of contentment, his body relaxing against mine.

Nothing had ever felt so right.

10

———

HAYDEN

It was a little hard to make out, but I thought the clock on the mantel read midnight as I blinked my eyes in the darkness. There was a soft glow from both the fireplace and the television that was still on after the movie had long since finished. The last thing I remembered was Buddy the Elf eating gum off a railing in NYC, so I hadn't made it very far into the movie before crashing.

After taking a nap earlier in the day, I was surprised I'd fallen asleep again, but as I lay there still wrapped in the warmth of Jonathan's arms, with the steady rhythm of his heartbeat against my back and his little puffs of breath ruffling my hair, I thought maybe I could see how I'd been lulled into sleep.

I'd told Jonathan I wasn't really a commitment guy, and that had been the truth, but it wasn't out of any sort of fear or unwillingness to try. I simply hadn't met a guy who'd been interested in any of that. College had been a time for exploring my sexuality and all the fun that came with it. And since then, I'd been more interested in trying to figure out my life than looking for a soulmate. I was only twenty-four. There was plenty of time for that later.

But lying in Jonathan's arms had me picturing a different sort of future. A dangerous one I had no business thinking about. Dreams of waking up in his arms, of lazy Sunday morning breakfasts, of trading sloppy blowjobs in the shower, would only serve to disappoint me when I went home in a couple of days. That's not what this was, and that wasn't our future.

Lips pressed against my hair and one hand stroked up and down my chest, eliciting a moan from me in response. He slid his hand underneath the hem of my shirt, tracing the same path up and down, only this time against my bare skin. I arched into his touch like a cat. God, I loved his hands on me.

His hand slipped lower, dipping below my waistband but not going any farther, instead moving side to side under the elastic. *Fucking tease.* I whimpered in response and ground my hips into his erection, trying to give him a taste of his own medicine, and was rewarded with a groan.

"Dammit, Lucy. You're killing me."

"One could say the same to you," he murmured into my hair, but his hand slid lower. Slowly. Painfully, excruciatingly slow until finally, the tips of his fingers grazed my aching cock.

"You started it," I gritted out, trying not to give him the satisfaction of a whimper or a moan. The asshole was going to pay for this.

One finger stroked the length of my erection, and it jumped in response. I was barely restraining my hips from punching up into his hand.

"Somebody likes that." I'd never heard him use a teasing

tone like that before, but I was too lost in sensation to give it any more thought.

Despite my best efforts, a whimper escaped as he gave me another torturous stroke with that single finger. His chuckle turned to a groan, matching mine, as he finally wrapped his hand around me.

"Please," I whimpered, begging him to do something, anything, to relieve the pressure building in my balls.

Fucking finally, he slid his hand up and down my length, but his movement was constricted by my sweats. Impatiently, I lifted my ass and yanked them down to my thighs in one motion before settling myself back in front of him, making sure to rub against his erection again for good measure. He was hard as a rock.

"God, you feel good," he said as he resumed stroking my shaft. He nudged my head, and I turned it to one side, giving him room to trail kisses down the column of my throat. He nipped at my ear, his breath hot and heavy against my already overheated skin, then whispered, "You going to come for me, Hay? You going to give me your load? How far up your chest do you think you can shoot?"

Those filthy words coming from his usually perfectly proper mouth had my balls drawing up tight. I was so fucking close.

"Lift up your shirt. I want to lick every drop of cum off your pretty chest."

Fuck. I hastily tugged my shirt up only seconds before I erupted, hot ropes of cum landing across both pecs and my abdomen.

Before I even knew what was happening, Jonathan slid out from under me, my torso flopping back on the couch. I watched as he yanked down his own sweats and began stroking himself furiously. Only a few short moments later, he shot, his cum mingling with mine across my torso. No one, and I mean, no one, has a good O-face, but somehow, Jonathan managed to look beautiful in the firelight with his head thrown back in pleasure.

Leaning forward, he dragged his tongue up my happy trail from navel to neck, lapping up our cum as he went. It was the hottest goddamned thing I'd ever seen.

I watched as he continued licking my chest, cleaning every last drop before leaning forward to kiss me. I loved the mingled taste of us on his tongue. It was erotic as hell.

Breaking apart, he stood, reaching his hand out to help me up. He led me into the bathroom, where we brushed our teeth before heading into the bedroom. He stripped completely naked and climbed into bed.

"Hay?" he asked, noticing my hesitation.

"Are you sure you want me in bed with you? I can sleep on the couch again."

He sat up, letting the blanket fall to his waist, exposing his bare chest. "Why wouldn't I want you here? We already took a nap earlier today."

"I don't know. This is just a casual thing, right? And I thought it might blur the lines."

His eyebrows rose into concerned arches. "Does it blur the lines for you?"

"No." *Yes.* "I know what this is."

He flipped back the comforter, and I crossed to the bed, undressed, and climbed in next to him, rolling onto my side, facing away from him. I didn't want him to see the confusion I was sure was swirling in my eyes.

"Usually, I'm the overthinker," he said as he pulled me back into him, his warm arms wrapped around me. Even as my brain tried to question everything, my body relaxed into him. He felt so damn good.

And despite my concerns, I was asleep in moments.

11

JONATHAN

December 25

I had never been so disappointed to wake up to an empty bed. I'd fallen asleep with Hayden wrapped in my arms, sated from mutual orgasms and comforted by his warmth. Now, I was lying in a chilly room with the sheets gone cold, and the only hint he'd been here was the scent of him on the pillow next to me.

I turned my head, shoving my nose into the pillow and inhaling deeply. I didn't think I could identify what it was in that scent that pulled me to him, but there was something about it that was comforting, like being wrapped in a warm blanket.

Jesus, what the hell was wrong with me?

I was probably the least sentimental person on the planet, besides my father, of course. Since when did I analyze the effect someone's scent had on me?

But good god, Hayden had had that effect on me since he'd walked into the cabin, what was it—not quite two full days ago. He made me feel like a different person. I'd experienced more emotions in thirty-six hours than I could remember feeling in an entire year, which was saying something as someone who'd just finalized his divorce. It was unnerving.

Though I also couldn't remember the last time I'd felt so good. And I wasn't just talking about the orgasms. Hayden had a way of getting me to not take life quite so seriously. To worry less and laugh more. To spend less time concerned with expectations and all the ways I should be acting and thinking, but instead, just live in the moment and take things as they came. It was freeing.

And terrifying.

That was enough of that. I threw back the blankets and rose from the bed, stretching my arms and admiring the view. Since there was no one out here in the wilderness, we hadn't bothered pulling the curtains the night before. The sun was shining on all the untouched snow, making me feel like I was in the center of a snow globe.

With the scent of bacon wafting in through the closed door, I pulled on my joggers from last night and stumbled out of the bedroom, wordlessly making my way into the bathroom to piss and brush my teeth. Looking at my reflection in the mirror, I almost didn't recognize myself. My usually tidy hair was standing on end, the stubble I hadn't shaved yesterday was even thicker today, and I could see the marks of a hickey at the base of my neck. I wasn't sure when Hayden had put that there, but to my surprise, I actually liked it. I liked that he'd marked me. That someone had wanted me badly enough to do it. I couldn't think of anyone, not a man or woman, who had desired me enough to mark me. To claim me.

God, what else had I been missing out on? What things had I discounted as unnecessary simply because I hadn't experienced them? I'd spent my whole life operating on all manner of assumptions. How many of them had been wrong?

I pulled the first aid kit out from under the sink and redressed the cut on my hand. It didn't look as bad as it initially had but was still a bit tender and sore. I found a large Band-Aid and managed to get it on one-handed, then left the bathroom.

I followed the scent of bacon and coffee into the kitchen, where Hayden was standing at the stove, manning a griddle and a spatula. I came up behind him, wrapped one arm around his torso, and placed a kiss just above the neckline of his T-shirt.

He leaned his head back against my shoulder for a moment, giving me better access to nibble on his neck. "Mmmm. That feels good."

"You taste good." I gave him one last nip before backing away and turning toward the coffee maker. "I can't believe you're up before me."

"I take it you're an early riser?"

"Usually. I've always been wired that way. Even as a kid."

"That tracks."

I turned and leaned against the counter opposite where he was flipping pancakes and sipped my coffee. "Why do you say that?"

He tossed a smirk over his shoulder before returning his attention to the griddle. "You just strike me as the sort of person who thrives on routine, and that would naturally include getting up early."

"You think you have me all figured out, do you?" I asked playfully.

He moved the pancakes to a plate and handed it to me. "Take these over to the table, will you?"

I took the plate he offered, along with my coffee, and moved into the dining area. Hayden followed with a plate of bacon, a mug of coffee, a jug of syrup, and the butter dish, all balanced precariously between his two hands. I held my breath as he set everything down, impressed that he'd managed not to drop anything.

We each took a seat, taking pancakes and bacon and piling them on the plates Hayden must have set out earlier. I shook my head as he drenched his pancakes in syrup, then dove in, mangling them as he cut his first bite. I, in turn, poured a strip of syrup, then cut a row into bite-sized pieces before lifting one to my mouth.

Hayden watched in amusement. He pointed at the neat rectangle-shaped bites on my plate and said, "You like order and structure. You definitely have a morning routine."

He wasn't wrong, and I wouldn't apologize for it. To my mind, an orderly life was a virtue. I hadn't had a successful career without structure and discipline. "Is there something wrong with structure in my day?"

"No. Not at all." He shoved another huge bite into his mouth. "It's just not how my brain works. Routine and structure are boring, so my brain decides to find something else more interesting, and the next thing I know, I'm twenty minutes late because I decided the books on my shelf need to be arranged by color. Then I notice three of the books are actually overdue library books, so then I have to go through all the books to make sure there aren't any other ones overdue. But then I can't remember where I set the first three, so I have to go looking for those, and then, somehow, I lose my car keys in the process."

My brain short-circuited just listening to that. "Is that...? How do you...? What?"

He laughed. "Right?" He leaned over and patted me on

the shoulder. "It's okay, Lucy. I'm used to it. But life would definitely be easier your way."

My pancakes sat untouched in front of me. I was at a total loss. "If you acknowledge structure and routine are easier, why don't you create a routine for yourself?"

He shoveled in more pancakes. It was kind of fascinating, actually, how he could continue to hork down pancakes at such a steady rate and still maintain a conversation. "Tried it. Didn't take. Tried it many times, actually. I can maintain a routine for a few days, but it never lasts, and honestly, the pressure of trying to keep it going is almost more stressful than just winging it the rest of the time."

I was starting to get a headache. "So you do get stressed out. You just seem like someone who is perfectly happy to fly by the seat of their pants without a care in the world."

"And that bugs you, doesn't it?" His words weren't malicious. Hayden seemed genuinely curious.

"I'm not sure how to answer that. I suppose, yes, maybe it does."

"You should eat those before they get cold." He pointed his fork at my plate. I picked up a piece of bacon and took a bite as he continued, "So here's the deal. I do get stressed. It's frustrating to lose things all the time. It seems I'm constantly looking for my keys or my wallet. I struggle to pay bills on time. Someone's always annoyed with me because I'm late. It even cost me a job back in college. Then, of course, there's the fact that I'm a total disappointment to my parents."

"I'm sure your parents aren't disappointed..."

"Oh, they are. Dad makes it clear just about every time he sees me. And Mom...she never really says anything, but I see the look she gives me when I show up late. Though I suppose with her, it's more worry than disappointment. And

Jon...well, he defers to my mom when it comes to me, but he's made it pretty clear he doesn't understand me. He barely even speaks to me."

"If it makes you feel any better, he barely speaks to me as well." My tone was dry as a desert.

He shrugged. "It's not really the point. And I'm not looking for pity." He was trying to brush it off, but I was starting to wonder if maybe it bothered him more than he let on, maybe even more than he realized. "I just learned a long time ago that I'm not wired like everyone else. And if I spend my whole life trying to conform to everyone else's expectations, I'm going to be miserable. So I forgive myself when I fuck up because at the end of the day, I'm doing my best, just like everyone else. I try not to let it get to me."

We ate in silence for a moment as I considered his words. He made it sound so easy. I didn't think I'd ever forgiven myself for a single thing in my life. I was brutally hard on myself. My need for structure was, in some ways, a need for control. If I could anticipate every way something could go wrong, I could get ahead of it before it happened. I could control the outcome and avoid failure.

But had it really worked? Things still went wrong. Wives still cheated. Marriages still failed.

"Maybe routine and structure aren't all they're cracked up to be."

He snorted. "Are you feeling okay? Has some sort of Dickensian ghost come to warn you about your future?"

"I've maintained the most orderly existence known to man, and my ex-wife still walked out on me. She said I was boring. Predictable."

"Oh, Lucy." He placed his hand on mine.

"Don't you fucking pity me."

Ignoring my comment, he squeezed my hand, then

leaned forward and grasped the other one so we were facing each other, both hands clasped. "You may be predictable, but you aren't boring."

I huffed. "Right. I believe Rebecca's words were, 'I'm wasting away in this marriage,' and 'The predictability is sucking the life out of me.'"

"Rebecca was a pretentious bitch who only wanted you for the status she thought you could provide. She just said those things because she couldn't come up with anything else to hurt you." His words were said with so much affront that they nearly had me smiling.

"She cheated on me," I admitted. I don't know why I hadn't told anyone in my family or why I was telling him now. Somehow, her infidelity felt like an indictment on my ability to make her happy. And no matter how many times I told myself her cheating couldn't be justified, I still harbored some sort of belief that it was just as much a failure on my part as it was on hers. "She cheated on me, and like a fool, I was still willing to work through it, but she twisted it around like it was my fault, like the way I lived my life was ruining hers." I stared at our clasped hands, unable to look at him while I confessed the rest. "And the worst of it is there's still a part of me that believes she was right. Like if I could have just been a little more agreeable, a little more flexible and less rigid, she wouldn't have felt the need to fuck someone else."

Hayden released one of my hands to tip my chin, forcing me to look at him. His chocolate-brown eyes were stormy and intense. "That's bullshit. None of that is your fault. None of it. She was just looking for a way to justify her own shitty behavior. You're not boring, Lucy. And for someone like me, who is followed by chaos wherever he goes, your adherence to structure and routine is comforting. I like knowing that no matter how much my brain spins out of control, you'll be right there, steady and dependable."

There was a little flutter in my chest at the thought of being there for him longer than today and tomorrow, that it was even possible he'd want me that way. But down that path lay madness. Even if our parents could ever get on board with us dating, we'd drive each other crazy. We were too different.

"Thank you. We should probably shovel out our cars after breakfast." I squeezed his hand and then tried to let go, wanting to return us back to stasis, but he wasn't having it.

"Don't deflect. I mean it, Lucy." He cupped my cheek, lightly stroking his thumb across my stubble, and I couldn't stop myself from leaning into it just a bit. "There is nothing wrong with you. And fuck her for suggesting otherwise. I like you just the way you are."

I closed my eyes, releasing a shaky breath. This conversation was too intense. Too intimate. I didn't know what to do with the feelings swirling inside me. It felt like I was spinning out of control. And I never, ever relinquished control of anything, least of all my emotions. I felt the press of his lips against my forehead and fought back the tears trying to break free from behind my eyelids. I'd be damned if I would let them fall.

Maybe he sensed he was pushing my limits, that my rope was about to break free of its mooring and I'd be endlessly adrift in a sea of emotions I wasn't capable of handling because he pulled away, wordlessly taking our plates in hand and moving into the kitchen. I remained in my seat, unmoving, trying to regain control of myself, grateful he allowed me the space to do so.

With all the dishes cleared, he stood in front of me once again, offering his hand to help me up.

"Let's go clean off our cars."

With relief that we weren't going to revisit the topic of my divorce, I let him pull me up. But before he took a step away from me, I pulled him into my arms. I didn't say anything more, and neither did he. We simply stood there and held each other.

12

———————

HAYDEN

We changed into winter-weather gear and made our way outside to go about clearing off our cars. Unsurprisingly, my decision to come up to the cabin had been an impulsive one, and my packing reflected that. I had nothing but joggers, hoodies, socks, and holiday-themed underwear, and the only shoes I'd brought were an old pair of Nikes. Not exactly snow-shoveling attire, but it would have to do.

Jonathan, of course, had donned snow pants, waterproof boots, and a thick winter coat. We both pulled on gloves and beanies, and Jonathan loaned me an extra scarf. Because, of course, he had an extra scarf. But whereas I previously might have rolled my eyes at his inexplicable need to over-pack and over-plan, I now was starting to understand that he did these things out of a need for control. And I sure as shit couldn't complain when it helped me out in the process.

The sun shone bright as we made our way outside. Temperatures had climbed to a balmy twenty-nine degrees, and with the sun shining, some of the snow had started melting just a bit. We trudged a path through the thick snow in the direction of the shed, off to the side of the cabin. Thankfully, the distance wasn't too far, though I had snow inside my shoes by the time I made it inside. After finding a shovel and a broom, we proceeded to make our way back toward the driveway, with me clearing our path with the shovel and Jonathan following behind with the broom.

I wasn't sure how effective he would be operating a broom with his left hand in the heavy snow, but I recognized his need to do something productive and get out of his head for a while, so I figured it was easier to just get it over with. Besides, I was starting to get restless in the cabin, so it probably wouldn't hurt to burn off some energy too.

Though I could think of other, more pleasurable ways to accomplish that.

I began working on clearing a path around each of our cars, hoping to make it easier for Jonathan to get to them to brush off the snow. Of course that meant I'd have to go around them all over again because the snow he brushed off landed right in the spots I'd just cleared. Too late to change course now, I kept at it, working up a sweat despite the chilly air.

As I worked, I kept thinking back to the way Jonathan had looked at breakfast this morning. I couldn't get the image of him looking so utterly broken as he'd told me what that bitch had said to him. I'd always thought of him as self-assured and totally unflappable, who never had to worry about being overrun with emotion and self-doubt because he knew who he was and didn't give a flying fuck what anyone else thought.

But as I'd sat there, listening to him talk, his voice so small, I'd realized he was just as human as the rest of us. He'd been hurt by a woman who hadn't valued the beautiful man he was. He was still hurting, in fact, though I was willing to bet he'd convinced himself he was fine. I'd wanted to pull him into my lap and kiss all that hurt away until he was my Lucy once again, serious and full of judgmental snark. Though that wasn't really who he was to me anymore. He was often serious and could definitely be judgy, but he'd also played drinking games with me, kept a copy of *Elf* in his stack of videos at the cabin, and had insisted on holding me while we slept last night. There was another side of him I thought he didn't let out to play very often, and for some reason, I was privileged to see it. I wanted to see more.

We'd been at it for about thirty minutes, me shoveling the driveway and Jonathan pushing snow off our cars with the broom, when I was pelted in the neck with a snowball.

"What the f—?"

Thwack. Another one hit me square in the back, followed by childish squeals of glee from the thirty-two-year-old man I'd had a discussion about routines and structure with just an hour ago.

As melting snow slid down my neck and underneath my hoodie, I wanted to be pissed, but the sound of his laughter, so pure and free, ringing out on a beautiful Christmas morning, had me smiling, even as I doubled over to make a snowball of my own.

I grabbed more snow on the run, laughing as I dove behind the other side of my car.

"Come on, Hay. You know you can't hide."

"Not fair, Lucy, hitting me from behind without warning."

"Aw, you'll be okay. I'm throwing left-handed. I figure that makes us evenly matched."

As he pursued me, I crept around the car slowly, moving

in the opposite direction of the sound of his voice, trying to settle on a strategy. I wasn't going down without a fight.

"You're saying you're so good that it's only fair if you fight left-handed? Or are you saying I'm that bad?"

"Don't take it personally. I played baseball in high school." I was momentarily distracted by images of him in a baseball uniform. *Fuck* that was hot.

I shook it off. His voice was getting closer, and if I didn't make a move, he would have me cornered between his car and mine.

"Did I forget to tell you? One of my obsessions in college was darts. I have excellent aim." Jumping up from my crouch, I launched a snowball at him and made a run for it, not bothering to see if I'd hit my intended target, and headed back down the path toward the shed.

I'd thought to seek cover behind the building, but I'd miscalculated and came face to face with Jonathan, who'd come from the other side. He grabbed my arms, pulling me into him before I could escape.

"Where do you think you're going?"

His cheeks were flushed with cold and exertion, and his eyes were alight with mischief. It was almost painful to look at him, like looking directly into the sun. And yet, as if I was a flower in bloom, I couldn't resist turning toward his warmth, basking in his joy.

He'd never looked so beautiful.

"I believe you started this. You've pelted me with snow, and you've trapped me behind the shed. Now what are you going to do, Lucy?"

"I'm going to kiss the shit out of you." He slammed his lips into mine, electricity snapping and popping between us in the chilly December air. Eagerly, I opened for him, accepting the onslaught greedily. He tasted like syrup and laughter, and I could have kissed him like that for hours.

"We're wearing too many clothes." His lips moved against mine as he uttered the words as if he couldn't bear to break contact long enough to speak.

"We should do something about that." I dove in for another kiss, not wanting to break the contact either.

Abruptly, he jerked away, grabbing my hand and tugging me down the path with purpose.

"You know we only got about half of the snow cleared..." I couldn't resist throwing that in his face.

"It'll melt." He glanced over his shoulder without breaking stride, tossing me a smirk with one eyebrow raised. "Eventually."

I laughed, loving every bit of this playful side of him. "What's gotten into you?" We stumbled into the cabin and began unwinding scarves and untying shoes, hastily trying to strip out of all our layers.

He kicked off his boots, then leaned over and kissed me on the nose. "It's Christmas. Maybe I'm tired of taking life too seriously. Tired of analyzing every step I take and looking for all the ways it could go wrong. Maybe I want to live a little more like you."

He leaned in to kiss me again, but I pulled back before his lips could touch mine. "What do you mean 'a little more like me?'"

He pulled back, a little wrinkle forming between his brows. "Carefree. Not worrying about the consequences of your actions. Just taking life as it comes."

I pulled back even farther so we were no longer touching. A drop of melted snow slid down my back, and I shivered. "Is that how you see me? As someone who doesn't care about the consequences of his actions? Someone who's thoughtless about others?"

He frowned and reached for me, but I took another step back. "Come on, Hay. You know that's not what I meant. I don't think you're thoughtless."

"But you do think I don't care about the consequences of my actions?" God, we were right back where we'd started two days ago.

"Don't twist my words." Waves of frustration rolled off him. "I never said you didn't care. I only meant that you didn't worry about everything all the time."

All the playfulness from just moments ago was gone completely. Instead, the air was thick with anger and frustration as we faced off against each other in the entryway.

"Oh, I see. I don't worry about things. Got it." I ripped off my beanie and peeled off my socks, which were soaked through from the snow that had slid into my shoes. "Well, I'm going to go *not worry* about the fact you're an asshole in the shower."

"Dammit, Hay! Don't walk away like that," he called out, but I waved him off, stepping into the bathroom and shutting the door.

13

JONATHAN

The click of the door to the bathroom closing echoed throughout the cabin. It felt like a death knell to whatever this was between us.

But I didn't want that. I wasn't done with Hayden, no matter that this was supposed to be a fling with an expiration date. We hadn't reached that date, and I wasn't ready to let him go, dammit. I was starting to think I wouldn't ever want to let him go. But that was future Jonathan's problem. For now, I needed to fix this.

I replayed the conversation we'd just had, trying to figure out where it'd all gone to shit. I hadn't meant to insult him. He wasn't thoughtless. In fact, he was incredibly thought*ful.*

But those had been his words, not mine. I hadn't said he was thoughtless. I'd said he was carefree. Why was that bad? To live life without having paralyzing anxiety over every decision one made sounded liberating.

Still confused, I crossed to the bathroom and knocked. I could hear the shower running and wondered if he was ignoring my knock or if he couldn't hear it over the sound of

90

the water. I tested the handle, and when it turned, I slowly pushed the door open.

The small bathroom had already filled with steam, heating the space and fogging the mirror. I quietly closed the door behind me and sat on the toilet.

"Hay?" I called cautiously. Something hit the floor of the bathtub, probably the bar of soap. "*Jesus. Fuck.* You followed me in here?"

"Help me understand where I went wrong. I didn't mean to upset you."

He pulled back the shower curtain just enough so I could see his face. His eyes searched mine for a moment. "You really don't get it, do you?"

At a loss, I shook my head.

He released a sigh, then said, "Get in here."

"You want me to get in the shower with you?"

"The hot water in this place doesn't last very long. I don't want to talk to you through this curtain, and I don't want the water to run cold while I stand here hashing this out."

I stood and stripped out of the rest of my clothes as quickly as I could with my injured hand. I pulled back the curtain and carefully climbed into the tub. It was a tight space for the two of us, but I didn't mind. It gave me an excuse to touch him, which I found I suddenly needed desperately, in a way I'd never needed from anyone else.

Hayden pulled me into him, hugging me close, and I closed my eyes, savoring the feel of him wrapped around me. "Why are you hugging me? Aren't you mad?" I asked against his shoulder.

"Do you want me to let you go?"

"No! Please don't." My voice held a needy quality I didn't think I'd ever felt before. Hayden was bringing out all sorts of new things in me. It was confusing.

I relaxed into him as he squeezed me even tighter.

"Do you know what people say when I run late all the time?"

"No."

"They say it's rude. That I'm selfish for keeping other people waiting or that I just want the attention. When, in fact, I feel terrible every single time. And like a failure because, once again, I've fucked up.

"Do you know what people say about the fact that I'm a server?" He didn't wait for my response. "I have no direction. No ambition. I'm too lazy to get a 'real' job and use my degree. I'm an ungrateful asshole because my parents paid for my education and I don't even use it.

"My room is messy, so I'm a slob. My bills are overdue. My car runs out of gas. I lock myself out of my apartment. I leave my laundry in the washer for three days without moving it to the dryer. I'm irresponsible. Forgetful. Lazy. Careless."

I ran my hands up and down his back as he got more and more agitated. We'd started out with him holding me, but I was pretty sure I was the one holding him now.

"Do you know how many times my father has said all those things to me? How many times he's accused me of not understanding the consequences of my actions?"

Ah. I was beginning to see where I'd fucked up. I didn't interrupt, though, wanting to hear Hayden out completely.

"Do you know how frustrating it is to have a messy brain? To be an adult and still feel like you don't have a handle on your own life, no matter how hard you try? To never be taken seriously because everyone around you assumes you don't take your own life seriously? I take meds, and they help a little, but it seems like no matter how hard I try, I'm letting someone down or causing someone inconvenience, and everyone else makes assumptions about all the reasons why."

I pulled back and looked at him, running my thumbs along his cheeks, catching the tears as they fell while the shower continued to run behind him. "That must be very frustrating."

He choked on a sob. "My brain is broken, Jonathan." How quickly I'd gotten used to him calling me Lucy. I didn't like him calling me Jonathan. Jonathan was the guy the rest of the world saw. Lucy was just for him.

"Your brain isn't broken. It's brilliant." I brushed a wet strand of hair back off his forehead. I hated that my words had hurt him so much. *I* was the thoughtless one. "I'm amazed by you. That you can deal with all of that and still be such a light in the world. You have a beautiful spirit."

"How do you know? You barely know me."

"You don't think I never noticed how you always light up the room? Every holiday, you're surrounded by people hanging on every one of your words. Smiles and laughter abound when you're around. I was always a little jealous that everyone seemed to adore you, whereas I always got barely more than a polite hello. There's a light inside you that shines on everyone in your presence."

"Why didn't you ever say anything?"

"What would I have said? 'I'm jealous that people like you more than me?'" Uncomfortable, I shrugged. "Besides, in some ways, it was a relief. I'm not great at small talk. I know I come off as cold and arrogant. With everyone's attention on you, I could sit quietly off to the side and stay out of the fray. It was best for everyone that way."

He leaned forward and pressed his forehead against mine. "We're quite the pair, aren't we, Lucy?"

There it was. Lucy. His Lucy. Thank god.

"I think we're both a little bruised and maybe a little scarred, but I think maybe we can also help each other move past it. I didn't even know I was carrying half this shit around until this weekend." I placed a kiss on his forehead and then pulled back to look into his eyes. "I'm sorry I upset you. You have such a sunny disposition. It just seems like you don't let anything get to you. I shouldn't have assumed that meant you didn't have things that worried you. I admire that you're able to keep such a positive outlook despite the challenges in your life."

"I just don't see any reason to mope about things you can't change. I hate that my brain works the way it does, but I'm not willing to spend the rest of my life resenting something I can't change. So I do my best to not let it get to me. But that doesn't mean I'm not aware that my actions have consequences and that I don't feel terrible when something I do or fail to do causes a problem for someone else. No one is more aware of any of it than me."

I caressed the side of his cheek. "I know that. I think you're amazing. And I'm so sorry I hurt you. Forgive me?"

At his nod, I leaned forward and pressed my lips to his in a kiss I hoped conveyed the depth of my feelings. Of how sorry I truly was and how much I admired him for his strength. Of how I thought I was starting to fall for him and how fucking terrified I was that this would be over in just a couple of days and that no one else would ever make me feel like this ever again.

The water began to cool, but neither of us moved, lips locked in a kiss for the ages. I ran my hands down Hayden's back to the globes of his ass and pulled him into me, gasping as our hardening cocks brushed against each other, sending sparks shooting through my groin.

The kiss deepened, moving from tender and emotional

to urgent and needy. As I continued to knead his ass, he shoved his hands into my hair, gripping the back of my neck and holding me to him as if he was afraid I was going to disappear. Tongues tangled and teeth clashed as we desperately fought for dominance under the chilly water. I moved my hand from his backside, over his hip, and around to his front, where I took both our cocks in hand. We groaned at the first stroke, and I feared I wouldn't last long.

Abruptly, Hayden pulled away, his eyes meeting mine with intensity. "What is it? Do you want to stop?"

"No. I want you inside me."

"Are you sure?"

"Absolutely. I want you to fuck me, Lucy."

I reached behind him and turned off the water. "I'll be damned if the first time I'm inside you is in a cold shower. I want you in bed."

14

HAYDEN

I leaned forward and kissed Jonathan quickly before turning and yanking back the shower curtain. We stepped out and dried haphazardly before racing each other to the bedroom. I thought I would remember the sound of his laugh in that moment, so open and free, for the rest of my life.

In the bedroom, he tackled me to the bed, straddling my thighs and swallowing my laugh in another scorching kiss. I trailed my hands all over his body, exploring every ridge and valley. I wanted to feel every inch of him.

Without breaking contact, Jonathan reached over to the side table, blindly rummaging through the drawer. By the sound of things, he wasn't having any luck finding what I assumed were a condom and lube. Impatient, I said, "I have supplies in the front pocket of my backpack and also in my dopp kit."

"You keep supplies in your backpack?"

"I may be a mess half the time, but I'm a fucking Boy Scout when it comes to sex supplies."

Grinning, he kissed me, then climbed off the bed and

ran to the bathroom, where I'd left my dopp kit sitting on the counter. I stroked my dick lazily while I waited, amazed at the changes in him over the last couple of days. It was like watching the sun come out after a storm.

I chuckled at his antics as he came sprinting back into the room and tossed the supplies on the bed, then climbed on. His smile turned lascivious as he tapped my knee. "Show me that pretty hole."

Oh fuck. A dirty-talking Jonathan was a dangerous thing.

I pulled my knees back, hurrying to comply. The intensity of his stare lit a fire inside me from the inside out. "You want that, Lucy? You want to sink that dick into my ass."

"Damn, Hay." He trailed a finger from the tip of my dick down over my balls and taint, moving so slowly that my eyes practically rolled back into my head. Finally, he rubbed the pad of his finger against my hole, making my whole body shudder.

He picked up the lube, slicked up his finger, and returned it to my entrance, pressing gently. Every bit of my focus was on that single spot on my body as his finger slowly entered me. I was so focused, in fact, that the feel of his mouth engulfing my cock took me completely by surprise, eliciting a deep groan at the dual sensations of his finger inside me while my cock was inside him.

He added a second finger and then a third, scissoring them as he stretched me while he continued to work over my cock with his mouth. I was nothing but sensation, a live wire dangerously close to bursting into flame. He located my prostate and tapped, and without warning, I erupted down his throat. "Shit. Fuck. Sorry. It just feels so fucking good."

He didn't respond with words, just kept tapping that

spot as my hips rutted into his face and he swallowed each spurt of cum.

"You taste good," he said, licking his lips as he pulled off. His hair was standing on end, his lips were red and a little swollen, and there was a bit of a flush in his cheeks. He'd never looked more beautiful.

"You going to give me that cock?"

"You still want it? Even after you've come?"

I leaned up on my elbows, making sure he could see my face. "Lucy, I've never wanted anything more."

Heat flared in his eyes, and he wasted no time grabbing the condom, tearing open the wrapper, and rolling it on. After slicking himself with the lube and drizzling a little more down my crease, he lined himself up and slowly began pushing in.

I bore down as he slid past the first ring of muscle, breathing out as my body stretched to accommodate his thick cock. He paused a moment, his eyes raised, checking in with me. At my nod, he pressed in farther until he was buried to the hilt. He leaned forward and pressed his forehead against mine as our bodies adjusted to the sensation of filling and being filled.

"You feel amazing, Hay. Nothing..." He swallowed and tried again. "Nothing has ever felt this good. I can't..."

"Shh. You feel good too. Don't overthink it, Lucy." I was overwhelmed with feelings, and I suspected he was too. It was confusing and wonderful and scary and unlike anything I'd ever felt before. But as used to Big Feelings as I was, this was on a different level. One that I suspected was several levels higher than anything he'd ever felt. "Just move, okay? I want to feel you moving inside me."

He lifted his head, eyes searing into mine, as he slowly pulled back, almost completely to his tip, before slamming back into me again. And again. Over and over, he pounded into me, an urgent energy surging through him that had my cock stiffening again. I wasn't sure it was enough to make me come a second time, but that didn't matter. It just felt so fucking good to be used by him.

Faster and faster, he moved, pegging my prostate expertly on every stroke, sending sparks shooting through my body. The sounds coming from him were feral and had my balls drawing up once again.

With a mighty roar, he buried himself deep inside me and stiffened as he unleashed into the condom. I was so fucking close to coming again myself and he hadn't even touched me. Desperate to relieve the ache that had built up once more, I reached between us and stroked myself. Three tugs were all it took to have me coming, the hot liquid spreading between us, covering my hand, my chest, and his abs.

He pulled out, quickly tied off the condom, and collapsed on top of me in a sticky, messy heap. I relaxed my legs, though still kept them loosely wrapped around his calves, and stroked his back as we both struggled to catch our breath.

Despite the mess between us, the weight of him was comforting. I stroked his sweaty hair, not wanting to let him go. I'd hold him forever if he'd let me.

I had to stop thinking like that. I was only setting myself up for disappointment.

Eventually, he rolled off me, lying on his side with his head on my shoulder. "You make me feel things I don't know what to do with." My heart lurched at his words. "I don't know how to process any of this."

"Do you want to stop?" I held my breath, waiting for his response.

"No, I don't want to stop. And I think that's what scares me the most."

We both showered again, taking turns with soap and shampoo on one another, neither wanting to stop touching the other until the water ran cold and we got out. We ate lunch, then retired to the living room, where Jonathan picked up his Kindle and I got out my guitar.

I fiddled with it for a bit, tuning the strings but not really knowing what I wanted to play. For the first time in my life, I felt self-conscious about playing in front of someone. Lucy tried to act like he wasn't listening, but I caught him glancing over a time or two, which did nothing to dispel my nerves.

I'd played in coffee shops and open mic nights without a problem, but there was something about playing in front of him—*for him*—that felt more personal. He'd said I was amazing the other day, but that was...before. Before we'd fucked. Before I started to feel...things. Music had the ability to open me up in a way that transcended words, which typically filled me with joy, but in this environment, with *him*, it made me feel raw and exposed. Vulnerable. This thing between us had an expiration date, yet I kept allowing myself to get further and further entwined with him. It could only end in disaster.

Annoyed with myself and needing to do something, anything, to get this jittery feeling out of my system, I closed my eyes and began to strum. I began with "Coventry Carol." It was a little more obscure, but I had always loved the use of the Picardy Third at the end of the verse. At the conclusion of that one, I moved into "Silent Night," only pausing briefly to glance at Jonathan before continuing. "We Three Kings" was next, followed by "O Come, O Come, Emmanuel." After about thirty minutes of playing, Jonathan abruptly set his Kindle down and moved to the end of the couch closest to where I'd dragged one of the stools over to sit on.

"You have all that memorized?"

I shrugged. "It's not that hard."

"I bet not everyone would say that. I had a terrible time memorizing piano when I was a kid."

"I guess it's always been pretty easy for me."

"Why don't you sing while you play?"

"I didn't want to bother you while you were reading." That was partially true. Mostly, it was because singing left me feeling even more vulnerable than playing my guitar.

"Will you sing for me now?"

"What do you want me to sing?"

"'The Holly and the Ivy?'"

I raised my eyebrows at that. "Um, yeah. I think I can do that one."

"Did I pick one you don't know?"

"No, I just didn't expect it. It's not as common."

"It was my mom's favorite. Or at least, I think it was. I remember her singing it when I was little. I think the year before she died."

I swallowed. Jonathan never spoke about his mom. I knew she had passed when he was young, but that was all I knew. I'd seen one picture of her with Jon and a baby Jonathan on a shelf in Jon's home office, but that was it. My mom hadn't really been able to tell me much about her when I'd asked once out of curiosity. Apparently, Jon didn't talk about her much either.

I swallowed, the pressure now feeling very heavy, and

began to strum. This request felt significant in a way I wasn't sure either of us fully understood. I fumbled through the introduction, a little flustered, then got control of myself as I began to sing. I could feel my cheeks heat, but I kept my eyes on his the entire time, forcing myself to overcome my nerves out of sheer stubbornness. Thankfully, my voice didn't betray me and came through strong and true as I sang.

The moment I finished, he leaned over and kissed me. "Thank you for singing for me. I don't have very many memories of my mother, and I'm not an overly sentimental person, but that song has always been special to me. You sang it beautifully."

"Thank you." I wasn't sure what else to say. I was overwhelmed and unsure and awkward and scared. I usually barreled through life at full speed, forgetting to think before acting, diving in headfirst and hoping for the best. That approach had gotten me into countless predicaments over the years—failing grades in school, arguments with my father, employment issues—but I'd always managed to overcome, optimistic I could somehow come out alright on the other side. I'd bring the grades up, apologize to my father, find another job. I was rarely scared because I always had the confidence I'd figure out a way to fix it.

But right now, with the way Jonathan was looking at me, I'd never been so terrified. He was looking at me like I was something special. Like maybe I meant something to him. And I realized that I wanted that more than I'd ever wanted anything in my life. But what would happen when it all fell apart? Because things in my life usually did. Because Jonathan and I were so different—in age, personality, and our worldviews. Because our parents likely wouldn't accept any of this. And how would I fix it this time? How would I fix the damage to our family? Or my own broken heart?

Needing to put some space between us, I stood and grabbed the guitar case. "I should probably get dinner started. You said you bought a chicken for roasting?"

Jonathan stood and faced me, eyes searching mine. "Are you okay?"

"I'm fine. Why wouldn't I be?" My voice cracked like that meme of Ross saying "I'm fine" from *Friends*.

He arched a brow at my obvious lie. "I don't know. You just seem...twitchy."

"What does that even mean?" I turned and placed the guitar in the case. "I told you I'm fine." I was gratified that I'd managed to keep my voice more even this time.

"Okay, well, why don't I help you with dinner?"

"No, that's alright. I've got it. You just relax with your Kindle."

I set my guitar in the corner and walked into the kitchen.

15

JONATHAN

I frowned as I watched Hayden walk away. Something was clearly bothering him, and though he'd denied it, I had a feeling it had something to do with what was happening between us. Though maybe that was me projecting my own feelings on the situation.

So much had happened in the last forty-eight hours, and I didn't understand any of it. How was it possible to fall for someone so quickly? Someone you'd already known for years but, as it turned out, hadn't really known at all. Someone you were starting to realize might hold the key to unlocking the best parts of you. How had any of this happened in just a couple of days? And what was I going to do about it?

Hayden rummaged around in the kitchen, pulling out the chicken, herbs, onion, butter, and lemon. Most of the things I'd bought at the grocery store had been your typical bachelor basics, but I'd bought the ingredients for roast chicken thinking that even though I was spending Christmas alone, I might want to at least have this one nice meal. I'd stood in the middle of the market, just a few miles away from the cabin, searching for recipes online. The one I'd chosen had seemed straightforward, but Hayden wasn't even using a recipe.

I pulled the stool he'd been using while he played back over to the counter and sat down, watching him work. He'd already preheated the oven and was currently deftly dicing an onion. He then went to work on the herbs, stripping leaves off stems and giving them a rough chop. He rummaged through some drawers, then produced a small grater. He picked up the lemon and grated the peel with expert precision, turning it a little with each swipe. He added some minced garlic, salt, and pepper and then mixed it all together with a couple of spoonfuls of butter from a tub I'd bought so I could make toast for breakfast.

I watched in amazement as he began to shove the butter mixture under the skin with his bare hands. It was messy, but the lemon and herbs smelled amazing. Once he was finished, he placed the chicken in the oven and then got to work on the vegetables.

I was impressed by the competency of his work, sure that preparing the chicken would have taken me twice as long, and though I hadn't tasted the final product yet, mine likely wouldn't have tasted nearly as good. He thought he was a failure, but only because he was measuring himself against the wrong stick. We all had been. He still hadn't told me what his college degree was in, but with the little bit I knew about his father, it was probably something related to business.

And I couldn't fault his father for that. Wasn't that how society measured success? With your business acumen? I was a corporate accountant, for fuck's sake, just like my own father. I actually happened to like it, and I was good at it. Numbers were logical and orderly. But that wasn't the point.

The point was that Hayden wasn't meant for that type of thing. The world of business would be stifling for him. And it had nothing to do with his intelligence. I had no doubt he could conquer the business world if he chose to do so, but what if he had the freedom to conquer something else? Something that he was passionate about?

Hayden wasn't meant to sit idle. He was meant to move. To create. To soar.

After watching his skills in the kitchen over the last couple of days, I was sure he could be a chef. But he'd said he'd gone through a cooking phase and then lost interest. He'd expressed a desire in becoming a professional musician, and I also had no doubt he could be successful in that as well. I'd be willing to bet he was an excellent server. He'd be constantly in motion, friendly with his customers, and probably pulled in great tips. Most people didn't consider that a successful career, but why not? If he enjoyed it, was good at it, and it was paying the bills, why shouldn't that be a measure of success?

"Do you like serving? At the restaurant, I mean?"

He paused in the middle of dicing potatoes and looked up. "I guess so?"

I chuckled. "Are you asking me or telling me?"

"I mean, yeah, I like serving. But why do you ask?" He picked up the knife and resumed chopping.

"Well, I was just thinking that if you want to be a musician, you could continue serving to pay the bills while you try to get the music thing off the ground."

"You really think I could be a musician?" I hated how much doubt leached into his question.

"I absolutely do. You're amazing. Do you want to go at it solo or join a band?"

"Hang on." He finished prepping the potatoes and

popped them into the oven with the chicken. After pouring out two glasses of wine, he handed one to me, still standing in the kitchen with the counter between us. I wouldn't have taken him for a wine drinker, but he'd done nothing but surprise me since he'd gotten here. I supposed I ought to stop making assumptions altogether and just enjoy him for who he was rather than who I thought he might be.

"So I don't want to be, like, some big rockstar or anything. I just want to play locally in coffee houses and bars and such. Maybe the occasional music festival. But I don't know if I can make a living at that."

"Could you do the server thing *and* the music thing? With both incomes combined, could you make a living?"

"I mean, I make pretty decent tips." He took a sip of his wine. "I actually do really well, if I'm being honest. But serving isn't really a career."

"If you make good money, why not? Do you enjoy it?"

"Yeah, I guess I do. I like people, and I like the challenge of trying to give folks a memorable experience. And I like that it's never the same two days in a row." He frowned as he twirled his wine glass on the counter. "But I have a degree in business. Shouldn't I be using it?"

Jonathan from two days ago would have said *absolutely.* But now, I just wanted Hayden to do what made him happy and fuck what anyone else thought.

"Why did you go to college?"

He raised his eyes back to mine, confusion at the question written all over his face. "I don't know. It was just always expected of me."

"You said you changed majors a couple of times. What were they?"

"Marketing, economics for, like, one semester, and then I finished with business."

"Did you enjoy any of that?"

"No. I hated all of it."

"If you hated all of it, why did you pursue it?"

He looked at me like I was an idiot, like I should already know the answer. And I was pretty sure I did, but I wanted to hear it from him. No more assumptions. "I knew it was what my father wanted. And probably Mom too."

"If you could have majored in anything else, what would you have done?"

He sipped his wine and thought for a moment, brow furrowed. "I honestly don't know. Music, maybe? But I'm not sure studying that formally wouldn't have sucked the fun out of it for me. I don't mind taking lessons and practicing, but all that other stuff—taking tests, and I don't know what else—would have made it feel like work."

"Do you have to have a degree to be a musician?"

"I don't know. Probably not."

"So go for it. Be a musician if that's what you want. But don't allow yourself to be limited by what everyone else expects of you."

He stared at me a moment, astonishment written on his features.

"That easy?"

"Well, probably not. I'm sure it's fucking hard. But if it's what you really want, it will be worth it."

"Would you do it? Ditch the corporate whatever-it-is-that-you-do and go, I don't know, own a goat farm in southern France?"

A laugh burst out of me at that. "Goat farm?"

"I don't know." There was laughter in his tone and a sparkle in his eye that I found so damn attractive. I wanted to chase his light to the ends of the earth. "I was trying to come up with something opposite of what you actually do."

"I assure you I have no interest in becoming a goat farmer, though I wouldn't mind a visit to the South of France." I finished my wine and set the empty glass in front of me. Hayden reached back for the wine bottle and refilled our glasses as I continued, "I'm a corporate accountant, just like my father. And despite the fact that it was exactly what my father wanted for me, I actually like my job. Rules and numbers make sense to me."

"It must be nice to be able to follow in your father's footsteps. I'm sure he's very proud of you."

I scoffed. "You know how rigid and controlling he is. Everything has to be done his way and on his timetable. I don't think I've done a thing to please him my entire life. The accountant thing was just expected, so what was there to be proud of? It wasn't like I'd done anything extraordinary. I'm just lucky I ended up liking it."

Hayden had paused with his wine glass lifted halfway to his face and was giving me an incredulous look.

"What?"

"You know you're just like him, right? Or at least up until a couple of days ago, I thought so."

"I am not." This conversation was taking a turn I didn't care for. We were supposed to be talking about him following his dreams.

"What time do you get to the office every day?"

"Seven." I didn't see what that had to do with anything.

"Every day?"

"Of course."

"What time does Jon go in?"

"I don't know. When I was still at home, he usually left around six-thirty."

"...so he could get to the office at seven."

"Probably. I don't see how that makes me just like him.

Many people like to get an early start to their day," I grumbled.

"Alright. Where do wet towels go after a shower?"

What the hell kind of question was this? "They get hung up on the towel rod."

"Never tossed on the floor?"

"Why in the world would anyone toss a wet towel on the floor? It won't dry properly, and then it starts to smell. And it'll leave a wet spot on the carpet, which isn't good for the carpet either. Plus, then you don't have a towel waiting for you when you get out of the shower the next day."

His shit-eating grin had my little speech stuttering to a stop and my mouth clamping shut. I was sure I was pouting, but I didn't care.

"Do you know how many times Jon gave me a similar speech in high school? You even said it with a similar tone of voice."

"Okay, well, the towel thing is just common sense. And my father and I may be alike on some surface-level things. Obviously, I like structure, routine, and order. But that doesn't mean I'm just like him in other areas. I'm not nearly as judgmental." He raised his eyebrow, which I ignored. "I... um...I like mushrooms, and he doesn't. And...I like soccer, which he says is incredibly boring." I was reaching, and I knew it, but I refused to face the truth. Hayden's gaze softened as I reached for a more plausible difference. I blew out a breath.

"You know what, I really don't need this. I was trying to help you, and you shoved this bullshit in my face. Let me know when dinner's ready." I picked up my glass and stormed off. Only in this tiny cabin, there wasn't anywhere to storm off *to*. So I took myself into the bedroom and slammed the door.

16

———————

HAYDEN

I watched him go, wanting to follow but unsure if he needed space. I lasted about thirty seconds before I followed him anyway.

I nudged open the door cautiously. "Can I come in?"

He was sitting on the edge of the bed, staring down at his wine, so I couldn't see his face. He shrugged, which I took as assent, so I came in and took a seat next to him. He immediately scooted over, leaving a few inches of space between us.

Ah, angry Lucy was petty.

"I'm sorry I pushed. I didn't mean to upset you. I have a lot of respect for Jon, and you as well. I was just trying to show you how similar you are, in the hopes that maybe you'd have a better understanding of each other."

"Didn't feel that way. Felt like shoving all my faults in my face."

I could see what he meant. But the fact was, Jon wasn't a terrible person, and neither was Lucy.

"There's nothing wrong with being orderly and prompt. I told you this morning that I like that about you. But you and your dad...don't take this the wrong way, but you have a tendency to only see one way of doing things. Any other way of looking at the world is wrong." The crease between his brows grew deeper, though he still refused to look at me, and he didn't respond. "I used to think you were judgmental, but now I'm thinking it's not quite as simple as that."

I took a chance and slid closer. This time, he didn't scoot away. Gently, I took the wine glass from him and set it on the side table, then took both his hands in mine. "Lucy, look at me." Slowly, he lifted his head and met my eyes. This sweet man. He'd always had a prickly exterior, but I thought maybe it was a defense mechanism. The truth was, he just needed a little love and care, and I wasn't sure anyone had ever given it to him.

"In my experience, judgmental people are often that way because they want to make themselves feel better by pointing out other people's flaws. But that's not the case with you, is it? You're not judging. Those people just don't make sense to you. So you come off as aloof, but really, it's that you don't understand them. Is that right?"

"I suppose it could be."

"I must confuse the shit out of you, yet you haven't been cold. You've just made an effort to understand me. I've never had someone take the time to try to figure me out. I'm a good time. The life of the party. I have plenty of friends. But my messy life was always a source of amusement. A quick and easy joke. And mostly I could laugh with them, because honestly, sometimes it *is* funny. But I've never had anyone in my life actually try to understand why I am the way I am. Your dad certainly hasn't, but *you* have."

"I'm sorry. He's a dick."

"He's not though. He just doesn't understand me. So he always let Mom handle everything because I was her kid, and I didn't make sense to him. But he still supported me. He didn't love the guitar thing, but he paid for the lessons. He even came to a couple of recitals. He bought me video games, gardening supplies, and whatever else I was into at the time. He wasn't much for a conversation about any of it, but he still supported me in the ways he understood. My dad paid child support and Mom has her own career. Jon didn't have to do any of that, but he still made the effort."

"Then why didn't he make the effort with me?" His voice was barely louder than a whisper.

"Oh, Lucy." I pulled him into me, wrapping my arms around him as he laid his head on my shoulder. "Did your dad ever *tell* you he was disappointed in you?"

Silence. Then, "Not in so many words. But he never told me he was proud of me either. He never said much at all."

"He probably assumed you knew. If you always did what was expected, then he never had reason to tell you there was a problem. And some people just suck at expressing themselves. But that doesn't mean he wasn't proud. When's the last time you visited his office at work?"

"I don't know. At least ten years ago, probably more."

"Last summer, Mom and I were going to have lunch, but she wanted Jon to come with us, and for whatever reason, it made the most sense for us to meet at his office and then go from there." I wasn't completely sure, but it felt like he was holding his breath as I spoke, as if he was afraid of what I was going to say. "He's got pictures of you all over his desk. High school and college graduation. A team picture of your baseball team. Your wedding photo. I guarantee that man is proud of you."

"He's never once told me he loved me. In thirty-two years, I've never heard him say the words." His voice was small and sad, and it broke my heart

"Have you told him how you feel? Have you told him you love him?" His silence was telling. "Maybe you need to be the one to take the first step."

A beeping sound came from the kitchen, startling both of us, and we pulled apart. "I'm going to go check on dinner. But, Lucy"—I brushed my hand against his cheek—"you should talk to your dad when we get back. Tell him how you feel." I leaned forward and kissed his forehead. "Thank you for supporting my music. And for trying to understand me. It means everything."

Dinner came out pretty tasty if I said so myself. We kept conversation to easier, less personal topics, telling stories of our childhoods and talking about the mundane aspects of our jobs. I knew a little about accounting from my college courses, but Jonathan found a way to make it actually sound interesting. It was evident he really did enjoy his work, and knowing him, I was sure he was good at it.

After dinner, we put in another movie—*Christmas Vacation* this time—and cozied up on the couch to watch under a blanket. As Chevy Chase and Randy Quaid loaded a shopping cart with lightbulbs and dog food, I struggled to focus. In the back of my mind, my thoughts bounced back and forth between our conversation about my job and possible music career and his relationship with his father.

I'd never once considered the possibility of being a server long-term, but he'd made some excellent points. Maybe not everyone needed a career. Maybe a job could be just that, a job. I enjoyed it. I was a people person who constantly needed to be on the move. Serving definitely checked those boxes. I made pretty good money, at least enough for me to live comfortably with my roommate and my old car from college. Though, if the proposal was successful, I'd probably find myself without a roommate pretty soon. Still, serving would allow me the flexibility to pursue the music thing. I probably could even afford to take some lessons again to strengthen the skills I already had. My dad wouldn't be thrilled, but I was used to that. I could weather that storm.

I was still amazed that this had all been at Jonathan's suggestion. Never in a million years would I have thought Lucy would have suggested something so seemingly unstable as a career path. But when I really stopped and thought about it, I shouldn't have been surprised. I'd accused him of making assumptions about me when I'd first arrived, but I'd definitely made my fair share of assumptions about him. And what I knew now was that Jonathan held a depth I'd previously been unaware of. He was a man who needed to know his own worth, at least in his father's eyes. And he'd made sure I knew mine too. I believed he genuinely wanted me to be happy, even if my path to happiness looked nothing like the one he would take.

Could it be possible he'd be willing to walk that path with me? Would he be willing to forgo convention and date his stepbrother, even if that meant the possibility of damaging his relationship with his father? A relationship that was shaky to begin with?

The longer I stayed here with him in this cabin, the deeper I got. Somewhere along the way, I'd started imagining what it might be like if we continued this thing between us. I'd been so convinced I could walk away unscathed. That we could fuck this out of our systems and entertain ourselves while we were stranded in the snow. But now, I was pretty sure I'd be all sorts of scathed. So, so scathed.

As the movie wound to a close, I found myself, once again, contemplating putting some distance between us. I was usually much more impulsive than this, racing into a situation without thinking about it, just taking life as it came. I supposed I'd already done that when we started this fling in the first place. But now, I was torn between what felt good right now and what I knew would be better for me in the long run.

We both stood, stretching after sitting for so long. He started to head toward the bedroom, but I didn't follow. "I'm, uh"—he turned to look at me—"I'm just going to sleep out here tonight." His eyebrows drew up in question, but he only said, "Oh. Okay."

I nodded, then ducked into the bathroom before I could change my mind. I brushed my teeth and used the bathroom, then came out to find him waiting outside the door. "All yours," I said lamely.

Who says shit like that?

He still looked confused as he slipped past me, shutting the door behind him. I took the opportunity to change into pajama pants and a T-shirt, then lay on the couch, leaving only the lamp on and covering myself with the blanket. God, this felt so awkward, but my self-preservation instincts had kicked in, and now I didn't know what else to do but follow through with sleeping on the couch.

He came out of the bathroom and paused outside the door. I could just make out his profile in the darkened cabin. He stood for several moments, the awkwardness increasing while my mind spun with possibilities of what he might say. Finally, he said, "Merry Christmas, Hayden," in a voice so soft I could barely hear him, then padded off in the direc-tion of the bedroom.

I clicked off the lamp and lay there, staring at the ceiling, contemplating how I'd gotten to this point. I was fairly sure I was halfway in love with my stepbrother, which was abso-lutely bonkers considering we'd only been here together for forty-eight hours, and I was absolutely sure it was my fault. Well, I could fix this. Or at least I could stop the bleeding. I'd just go home tomorrow. Quite a bit of the snow had melted today, and we'd mostly cleared the cars off. I'd go home a day early, spend most of the trip feeling sad, eat a carton of ice cream under a blanket on my couch, and then be back at work the following day, everything back to normal.

The door to the bedroom opened, light spilling out into the darkened cabin. "Hay?" Lucy called tentatively. I really should go back to calling him Jonathan. "Are you still up?"

"Yes." My voice cracked, and I cleared my throat, repeating myself more clearly. "Yes. I'm awake."

I heard his footsteps approach the couch, and then he was looming over me in the dark. "Will you come to bed with me?"

I peered up at him, blanket tucked all the way to my chin. "I don't think that's a good idea."

"Why?" He sounded so bewildered that I could already feel my resolve slipping.

"I think I'm going to go home tomorrow."

He came around and sat on the edge of the couch near my hip, where there really wasn't room for both my body and his, yet I still scrambled to move as far in as I could to make space for him.

"Why? I thought you were going home on the twenty-seventh?"

His voice held a tinge of panic that was endearing yet

made all of this so much worse. Hope was a dangerous thing.

"I just think our lines have gotten crossed here, Lu—Jonathan. This was just going to be a fling, right? Well, it doesn't feel like a fling anymore, and I'm afraid one of us is going to get hurt."

"I don't like it when you call me Jonathan."

"Out of all of that, you focused on the name I call you?"

"I don't like it. Everyone calls me Jonathan. Jonathan is serious. He's organized and on time and boring as fuck. Lucy is...fun. He's silly and sexy, and he doesn't worry so much about every goddamned thing. I want to be your Lucy."

Oh, dear god. How was I supposed to do the right thing here? My throat was thick with emotion, the backs of my eyes burning with unshed tears.

"What's going to happen when we go home? Are we going to keep doing this? Are we going to announce to our family that we're dating? How's that going to work?"

He fumbled with the blanket, digging around until he uncovered my hand, then grabbed it in his, holding it tightly. "I don't know what's going to happen. I don't fucking know. I just know that imagining life without you right now...hurts. It fucking hurts, and I'm scared. I'm scared of losing you, and I'm scared of keeping you." He brought my hand to his lips and kissed them before resting his forehead against my fingers. "Mostly, I'm scared of losing you."

"I'm scared too," I whispered.

"Give me more time, okay? Give me tomorrow while I figure shit out. Please? I'm not ready to watch you go."

Every last bit of resolve was smashed to smithereens as I swallowed past the lump in my throat. "Okay, Lucy. I'll stay. One more day."

"Thank god." He kissed my hand again, then stood without letting it go. "Will you come to bed now? We don't have to do anything but sleep if you don't want to. I just want to hold you."

"Yeah." I tossed the blanket off me, untangled my legs, and stood. "I'll come with you."

I was afraid I might follow him anywhere if he'd let me.

17

JONATHAN

December 26

I woke to sunlight streaming in through the windows and a sleeping Hayden wrapped in my arms. I'd lain in bed for hours after he'd fallen asleep, savoring the feel of him in my arms and wondering what the hell we were going to do about this situation between us.

I was nothing if not a champion worrier, so my mind had managed to conjure up every possible way this thing between us could go south. We were so different. Our parents would never accept it. Society would never accept it. He would get discovered by a record label, become famous, and want nothing to do with me.

But for every one of those disastrous imagined scenarios, I'd come back to just how right it felt with him. Yeah, we were different, but we also complemented each other. Wasn't there something to the saying "opposites attract?" Our parents would accept us, or they wouldn't, and damn, I hoped they would, but if I had to choose between Hayden and our parents' approval, I'd choose Hayden every time.

And that's really what it came down to. Life without Hayden was no longer an option.

I just had to convince him of that.

I pressed a kiss to his shoulder, allowing my lips to linger there before moving a half inch and repeating the gesture. I continued in this way, lazily pressing kisses across the ridge of his shoulder, enjoying the way the heat of his smooth, sleep-warmed skin felt beneath my lips. As I pressed one more kiss to the base of his neck, right where it met the curve of his shoulder, he breathed deep, coming awake and sighing contentedly. I smiled against his skin, enjoying everything about this moment. The simplicity and pleasure of waking up next to someone you were into. Leisurely taking the time to savor and feel and enjoy without allowing worry and stress to intrude.

He rolled halfway onto his back, just enough so he could look at me with lazy eyes.

"Good morning," I murmured, pressing kisses along his stubbled jawline.

"Mmmm. Good morning to you." I felt his smile underneath my lips as I continued my way down to nibble on his ear.

"How'd you sleep?" I asked, licking the spot just behind his ear. He practically purred like a cat. "I slept like the dead."

"Good." More kisses down his neck, back to where I'd started this exploration. "I like waking up next to you."

"Do you?" There was a tinge of...something in his question, but I couldn't pinpoint what it was.

"Absolutely." My hand, which had slipped when he'd rolled over, tightened against his chest, pulling him against me, his back to my front. My hard cock was nestled into the crevice of his ass, with only our briefs separating us. I wondered what holiday-themed pattern was on his today. I hadn't been paying attention when we'd changed after our shower yesterday. I canted my hips, nudging his crack, and he whimpered, pushing back into me in return. "I could wake up to you like this every morning."

He froze, and I tightened my hold, afraid he was going to bolt. My words were bold and reckless and probably really fucking stupid. But where had measured caution gotten me before? I didn't know what our future held, but I knew I wanted more of whatever this was. I wanted to chase the good and fuck all the rest.

"Don't say shit like that, Jonathan." His voice was strained as if he was trying to hold back some emotion.

"I told you to call me Lucy."

He released an exasperated sigh. "Lucy, then. Don't say shit like that in the heat of the moment if you don't really mean it."

I released my hold on him so I could turn his chin back toward me. I wanted him to see the truth in my eyes. "What makes you think I don't mean it?"

His eyes flicked back and forth between mine. "You're serious?'

"I meant every word."

"But what does that mean?'

"I thought I was the overthinker here?" My attempt to lighten the mood didn't land.

"I'm serious, Lucy. What did it mean?"

I kissed the tip of his nose, then pulled back. "It means that I love the way it feels to have you sleeping in my arms. To wake up to you and make lazy love with the sun streaming through the windows, lighting up your beautiful body. It means I want more of this. More of you."

"Since when did you become such a damn poet?"

"Since I started falling for you."

"You're falling for me?"

I nodded slowly.

His eyes widened and he lurched forward, pressing his lips so fiercely to mine that he nearly knocked me off the other side of the bed. I rolled to my back, catching him as he attempted to straddle my hips, his feet getting tangled in the blankets. He kicked out in frustration, which only seemed to make the covers cling more stubbornly to his limbs. I chuckled and grabbed hold of him, forcing him to still his movements before he did something disastrous, like knee me in the junk.

"Take a breath, Hay. You're never going to get untangled if you thrash about like a fish caught in a net."

The sound he made could only be described as a harrumph, which was adorable as fuck, but he took my advice, reaching down more calmly to extricate himself from the blankets before settling back down on top of me, straddling my hips.

"Better?"

"You tell me." He dragged his length against mine at an excruciatingly slow tempo, eliciting a groan as a jolt of pleasure coursed through me. "Christ, Hay. Do that again, and this will be over before it starts."

"Serves you right for mocking me." The playful twinkle was back in his eye, sending almost as much warmth through me as when he'd rubbed against me a moment before. Taking each of his ass cheeks in hand, I pulled him against me, rocking into him, both of us whimpering at the friction. "C'mere." I released one of his cheeks so I could pull his head toward mine. "I want to taste you."

He came willingly, licking into my mouth in a sloppy kiss, teeth clacking in our haste. I shoved both my hands under the waistband of his briefs, kneading his ass as we rutted against each other. Abruptly, he pulled away and climbed off the bed. Before I knew what was happening, he yanked my underwear down, ripping them off my feet and tossing them on the floor, then did the same to his own before climbing back onto the bed. "If we're going to have a frotting session, we're going to do it right."

"Oh, is that what we're going to do?"

"Did you have something else in mind?" He didn't wait for a response. Just leaned over and snagged the lube out of the drawer, popping the cap and drizzling the silky liquid over both of us. I hissed as the cool temperature of the lube hit my overheated dick, but that quickly turned into a moan as Hayden slid his cock against mine. "On second thought —*fuck*—frotting is perfect."

He chuckled as he leaned forward, changing the angle and trapping our dicks between us, adding the additional friction of our abs as we rubbed against each other in slow strokes.

He brought his lips to mine once again, stubble scratching against mine as we kissed. I loved the masculine feel of him. The hard lines and angles, the rough feel of his body. God, he lit me up in ways no one—man or woman —ever had.

I met his tongue thrust for thrust as our hips matched the rhythm of our mouths. Languid thrusts transformed into frantic strokes as we rutted against each other, desperately chasing our release. My body was on fire, consumed by sensation at each and every point of contact with him. I wrapped my legs around the backs of his thighs, wanting to pull him even closer as if I could somehow fuse us together. Our bodies were slick with sweat, breaths panting, grunts and nonsense falling from our lips, abs slick with precum as our dicks leaked like crazy.

Hayden's strokes stuttered and his entire body stiffened as he threw his head back in ecstasy. I didn't have time to appreciate the beauty of him before my own orgasm barreled through me. I slammed my eyes shut, my load spilling between us, mingling with his, hot and sticky between our bodies. It felt like it went on forever, spasm after spasm coursing through me, even after he collapsed on top of me.

He rolled off me, settling his head on my shoulder and tossing one leg over my thigh as we both came down from the rush of our orgasm. The silence stretched between us, and I began to worry. It wasn't like Hayden to go so long without speaking, and I worried my declaration a bit ago had been too much for him.

"You okay?" I threaded my hand through his hair, nervously awaiting his response.

"This is all just happening so fast," he said quietly. "One second, I'm floating on cloud nine, and the next, I'm terrified it's all going to come crashing down."

I continued to run my hand through his hair, playing with the strands. "If it makes you feel any better, I'm scared too."

He finally pulled his head up to look at me, disbelief etched into his features. "You are?"

"Of course I am. You're talking to the guy who never makes a move without analyzing it from seventeen different directions. This is happening fast for me too."

"How are you so okay with it, then?"

"It's actually pretty simple. I mean, it's really not. It's complicated as hell." I ran my hand along his cheek. "But what it boils down to is that when I think about going back to my regular everyday boring life, and I imagine it without you in it, I find that far scarier than all the rest of it."

"Oh shit, Lucy. When did you get so romantic?" Finally, I saw the hint of a smile turning up his lips, and relief flooded me.

"It's not romance, Hay. It's just the truth."

18

HAYDEN

Jonathan came up behind me and pressed a kiss to the center of my neck as I stood in front of the sink, brushing my teeth. We'd showered, taking as much time to clean each other as we dared before the water turned cold again. He'd been tender and sweet as he washed me, saying very little as he took care of me. It made me feel treasured.

"I want to spend the day with you," he said, meeting my eyes in the mirror.

"I told you I'd stay today."

"No, I mean, I want to get out of the house. Go into town and explore. Maybe grab a bite to eat." He wrapped his arms around me from behind and rested his chin on my shoulder. "It looks like the driveway is mostly melted. We shouldn't have any problem getting one of our cars out."

"You want to take me on a date?"

His smile was shy like he was a teenager asking out a date for the first time. It was endearing. "I guess you could call it that. Is that okay?"

Warmth spread from the center of my chest, radiating outward and across my face in the form of a wide smile. "I'd love to spend the day with you." I turned in his arms and kissed him deeply but pulled back before it could turn dirty. "How soon do you want to go?"

"Whenever you're ready."

We finished getting ready, Lucy dressed in crisp jeans and a sweater over a button-down while I wore joggers and a hoodie—staples of my personality—and a ball cap backward over my overgrown hair I'd meant to have cut before the holiday but had forgotten. Again.

I was once again struck by how different we were, but I was trying not to hyper-focus on that and simply enjoy the time I had with him for as long as he wanted me.

We made the twenty-minute drive in his Audi without incident. The roads were fairly clear, though the trees were still blanketed in snow, and with the sun shining, the landscape was nearly blindingly white against the pure blue sky.

Since the cabin belonged to Jonathan's side of the family, I'd only been up here one other time and hadn't really explored the town other than to pick up grocery staples. My breath caught as we pulled onto Main Street. It looked like something straight out of a greeting card. The storefronts were clad in brick, stone, and wood, each one unique, with windows displaying post-Christmas sale items. Evergreen garlands hung from one side of the street to the other, with red bows adorning them, zig-zagging the length of the street. I hoped we would be here long enough for dark to fall so I could see everything lit up for the holiday.

After driving the length of Main Street—the equivalent of about one city block—Jonathan found a parking spot near what looked to be a small café. We popped in and ordered coffee and pastries, which we ate at the only table in the shop, tucked into a corner near the back.

"Tell me a story about your childhood. Something about the cabin or this town. We've talked about your dad, but I've never really heard you talk about anyone else in your family." I was careful to avoid mention of his mom specifically, as I'd only ever heard him bring her up one time and suspected that was a sensitive topic, but I knew he had other family, and I wanted to know more.

He thought for a moment, nibbling on a bite of his cinnamon apple muffin that was leaving crumbs everywhere. Every couple of bites, he'd sweep the crumbs into a neat little pile with his hands. He did this so efficiently, almost absentmindedly, that I was sure it was just something he did without thinking, like it was hard-wired into his DNA to make sure all messes were promptly taken care of.

"Grandpa Sam was my father's polar opposite. They drove each other crazy, but I found him absolutely fascinating. My mother died when I was four, so it's been just me and my dad for as long as I can remember. As you've pointed out"—he raised an eyebrow at me—"my father and I are quite similar, so I found it endlessly fascinating to see someone so...different from us. Grandpa was brash, cursed like a sailor, and laughed louder and more often than anyone I've ever met."

He sipped his coffee, then continued, "He owned a chain of shoe stores in the city that did moderately well—well enough that he was able to build the cabin out here when I was eight or nine, I think. After that, I'd come out here with him a couple of times a year, usually once in winter and once or twice in summer, sometimes for a weekend, sometimes longer. We'd hike or fish or just hang out at the cabin, playing board games, watching movies, or reading books. I hated the fishing but didn't really mind the hiking, and I always enjoyed listening to his stories. I think it was the only time in my life I was allowed to be a kid. I could spill stuff, leave clothes on the floor, and track dirt into the cabin, and he never batted an eye."

A shadow passed over his face, taking the joy with it.

"When did you last see him?" I placed my hand over his, trying to offer comfort.

"About seven years ago. He'd been sick with colon cancer, and I got permission from his doctors to bring him up here for a long weekend. Convinced them that some fresh air would be good for him. We spent the weekend just as we had when I was a kid, playing games and reading by the fire. He told me stories, and his eyes twinkled like they had when I was young. He passed about a month after we got back."

I stroked the back of his hand with my thumb, allowing him some space to lose himself in his memories. "The cabin is actually mine. Did you know that?" I shook my head in the negative. "He said my father was too practical and would probably sell it off rather than try to maintain it from the city, so he left it to me. It's been my retreat ever since."

Guilt washed over me. I'd come up here completely unannounced, running from a fight with my father, not giving any thought to the fact that Jonathan might be up here or that I'd intrude on his need for time alone. The only other time I'd been up here had been with Mom, and it hadn't ever dawned on me that the cabin wasn't Jon's.

"I'm sorry I crashed your weekend. I didn't realize the place was yours and didn't think before I came up here. I didn't even tell Mom I was coming. I was just looking for an escape and remembered coming here years ago and figured with them out of town, it would be empty. I shouldn't have assumed." I was babbling, frustrated that, once again, my impulsive behaviors had caused someone else inconvenience.

"Shhh. It's okay." He flipped his hand over, entangling his fingers with mine and squeezing. "I'm glad you're here. I came up here to wallow in self-pity over the fact that my marriage was over and I didn't have anyone to spend Christmas with. I probably would have finished that bottle of bourbon by myself and ended up eating cereal for dinner rather than cooking any of the meals I purchased groceries for. Instead, I've been gifted numerous orgasms, eaten several fantastic meals I didn't have to prepare myself, and have laughed more often than I can remember at any other point in my life."

He released my hand, leaning forward over the table and cupping my chin. "I don't regret a moment of the time I've spent here with you. In fact, I can't remember a better Christmas."

I closed the distance between us, pressing my lips to his. Aware that we were in public, I kept it chaste but still did my best to infuse as much feeling into it as I could. "Thank you."

"For what?"

"For saying that. For making me feel like I matter. Like you want me here."

"You do matter." He kissed me. "And I do want you here." He kissed me again, then stood, sweeping the crumbs from both his muffin and my Danish into his hand, then walked over to dump them in the trash, along with the wrappers. I followed with our coffees, handing him his, then zipping up my coat before we headed outside.

"Where to next?"

He held out his free hand, and I took it, savoring the feel of it wrapped in mine as we stepped out into the chilly December air.

"I have no idea."

19

JONATHAN

I reveled in the simple pleasure of strolling hand in hand down the sidewalk with the guy I was pretty sure I was falling for. I hadn't ever been much of a hand holder. At least, I hadn't typically been the one to initiate it, but right now, at this moment, I was enjoying the feeling of our fingers laced together, palm against palm.

I nearly ran into Hayden as he came to an abrupt halt in front of a storefront, but before I could process what type of store it was, he was tugging me inside. I giggled—fucking *giggled*—when he stopped just inside the door and I nearly ran into him again. "What has gotten into you?" I asked, my voice filled with laughter. It was ridiculous how much I laughed when I was with him.

Rather than answer, he stepped aside, revealing what my nose had already been trying to tell me. We were in a bookshop. A picture-perfect, small-town bookshop, complete with a cat sleeping on a chair in the corner.

The smell of books mingled with coffee and vanilla, the scents almost cloying yet somehow comforting in the small space. I was absolutely delighted.

It had been years since I'd been in a bookstore, primarily preferring the convenience and efficiency of my Kindle. But there was something so comforting about the smell and feel of physical books that I wondered why I'd stayed away for so long.

I chose an aisle at random, brushing my fingers along the spines as I walked. I favored fantasy and sci-fi but was delighted when I stumbled across an entire section of shelves devoted to queer romance. I plucked one at random, walked over to one of the cozy mismatched chairs in the corner, and sat down.

Hayden followed, sitting in the chair next to me. I couldn't make out the title of the book he'd chosen, but he grinned and cracked it open.

I lost track of time, noticing in an absentminded sort of way that Hayden got up and sat down a couple of times while I was deeply engrossed in a book about a college student caring for his dying mother, who was trying to convince a broody barista to go out with him.

"Do you think maybe you should just buy the book?"

I looked up, nearly having forgotten where I was for a moment. I smiled sheepishly at being caught so engrossed. "It's really good." I nodded toward the pile of books in his lap. "What did you find?"

"I'm a total mood reader and never know what will hold my attention, so I often have several books going at once. I grabbed several romances, a couple of fantasies, and one book about Eric Clapton."

It was so perfectly Hayden, and rather than lecture him about only sticking with one book at a time, as Judgey Jonathan might have done in the past, I simply stood, kissed him on the temple, and said, "Let's go pay."

❄

We spent a pleasant afternoon exploring the shops on Main Street, walking hand in hand, pointing out this item or that in storefronts as we passed. Hayden picked up some sheet music in a little mom-and-pop music store, which looked like it also served area schools. Band instruments were on display alongside guitars and electric keyboards, and there was a small repair shop housed in the back. The selection of sheet music was small, but Hayden still found some things of interest while I plunked out a melody or two from memory on one of the keyboards.

I purchased a couple of new ties in a men's clothing shop and contemplated a new sweater but ultimately decided against it. There were several shops owned by local craftsmen featuring handmade items we admired. In one shop, Hayden bought a necklace for his mom for Christmas, having put off his holiday shopping until the last minute, and in another, I purchased a handmade chess set for my father for his birthday next month.

By late afternoon, we were famished, having not eaten anything since our midmorning pastries. As far as we could tell, in addition to the bakery, the town's only other dining establishments were a diner back off the highway, an ice cream shop, and a bar and grill. We both agreed that a beer and a burger sounded great, so we headed in the direction of Billy's Bar and Grill, at the end of town opposite where we'd parked.

The hostess seated us in a booth off to one side, near the windows, giving us a pretty view of the snow-covered forest beyond. The restaurant itself was a combination of heavy wood and brass, with walls painted forest green, covered in photos and memorabilia from local high schools and the community college a couple of miles away. The U-shaped bar in the center of the space was surrounded by TVs, and since it was Sunday, all were tuned to football.

Our server greeted us, and we each ordered beers and double bacon cheeseburgers, his with tots and mine with fries, before settling back on either side of the booth.

A pall began to descend as I realized our day was winding to a close and he'd be leaving tomorrow. Typically, on a Sunday, I'd be dreading going to work the next day, but on this particular Sunday, it was the loss of Hayden I was dreading.

I reached over and grabbed his hand, holding it across the table. He looked at our joined hands, then up at me, his eyes widening in surprise. "Is this okay?" We'd been holding hands all day. I wasn't sure why it would bother him now.

"Yeah." He squeezed my hand. "It's more than okay. You just don't seem like a 'hold a date's hand in a restaurant' sort of guy."

"I'm not, really." I shrugged. "But I like holding yours."

He rewarded me with a shy smile, something I'd seen more of in the last day or so. He'd always appeared so confident, the life of the party at family gatherings, but just between us, he had shown a vulnerable side. I wasn't sure if that was a good thing or not. I wanted him to be free to be himself with me, for him to show me all his amazing facets, but I also hated to see him doubt himself. To doubt *us*.

"Today's been a good day."

"Yeah, it really has." He smiled wide, and I couldn't help but smile back.

"I want to keep seeing you when we go back to the city. I think there's something between us, something more than sex, that's worth exploring."

His cheeks flushed above his scruff. "I'd like that too." He ducked his head, fiddling with the cardboard coaster. He abruptly put it back down as our server arrived with our beers. We each took a long pull, and I sensed he was gathering himself to ask something. "So, are we, like, boyfriends?"

Warmth spread through me at his question. I hadn't really thought about labels, per se, but I liked the idea of being exclusive. Of being able to call him *mine*. "Yeah, if you're okay with it?"

"Um, yeah. I'd love that, actually. I've never had a boyfriend before."

"What? How is that possible?" Everyone loved Hayden. He was hot as fuck. How was it possible he'd never had a boyfriend?

He shrugged, setting his beer back down after taking another drink. "I don't know. I came out in high school, and it wasn't a big deal. I never really dealt with bullies about it or anything, but there weren't a lot of other out kids at school, so I only did a little light dating. Never anything serious, mostly just fumbling around in the back of a car. In college, there were a few guys I went out with more than once, but again, it was never anything serious, mostly just sex."

I hated thinking about him having sex with anyone. It made me want to punch someone.

"You're scowling."

I deliberately relaxed my features. "I don't like thinking about you with anyone else."

He laughed. "Did you think I was a virgin when I got here?"

"Obviously not, but I also hadn't given any thought to your dating history."

"I didn't like seeing you with Rebecca," he countered.

"How many times would that have been? Three or maybe four if you count the rehearsal dinner and wedding?"

"Probably. Didn't like it any of those times. I might have had a small"—he pinched his fingers together with just a tiny bit of space between them—"tiny, minuscule-barely-worth-mentioning crush on you in high school."

"Oh realllllyyy." I drew the word out, teasing him. I was delighted with this bit of information.

"I was seventeen, so you were what? Twenty-five? You were like this super smart, hot, older guy. I knew it was never gonna happen, but it didn't stop me from imagining it." God, that was both hot and embarrassing at the same time. He shrugged. "I was over it by the time you married Rebecca, but still. I never did like seeing you with her."

Our server brought our food, pausing our conversation.

He stole one of my fries and stuffed it into his mouth, then proceeded to drown his burger in ketchup. It continued to amaze me how things I once would have rolled my eyes at were now so adorable. Well, that wasn't entirely true. I was still rolling my eyes, but now it was in a good-natured sort of way.

"Let's stop worrying about everyone who came before and focus on us now and in the future."

He paused in dispensing his ketchup and looked at me with wide doe eyes. "You say the sweetest things. How do you do that?"

It was my turn to shrug, feeling a little vulnerable myself. "I'm not trying to. I just...when I'm with you, my feelings just come tumbling out. You've opened me up in a way I didn't think was possible. It's fucking uncomfortable if I'm being honest."

He laughed. "Good!"

"Good?" I raised one eyebrow.

He finished with the ketchup, then picked up his burger, poised to take a bite. "You've got me rattled, Lucy. Off-kilter. I'm glad I do the same thing to you."

"Wow. Thanks." I said it with sarcasm, but he was right. It was nice to know we were in this together.

20

———

HAYDEN

We passed the ice cream shop on our way back to the car, and I tugged Lucy inside, despite being full from dinner. I got a scoop of raspberry and a scoop of double chocolate piled high in a waffle cone. Lucy chose a modest scoop of vanilla in a cup.

We walked slowly as we ate. Temperatures had dropped as the sun went down, so we should have been hustling back to the car to get out of the cold, but I thought neither of us wanted to rush the end of the date. I certainly didn't.

The Christmas lights had come on now that it was dark, giving the street a festive glow, and it was just as pretty as I imagined it would be. The cold helped keep my ice cream from melting too fast. However, my hands were now really cold, and I thought I'd once again overestimated my ability to consume a large quantity of ice cream. I was starting to become painfully full, but the ice cream was so good that I couldn't stop myself. In between licks, I contemplated our relationship status.

Boyfriends.

My heart fluttered at the term. Seventeen-year-old me

could have never imagined it. However, now that it was our reality, I had some concerns. Were we taking this public? Were we telling our parents? How often would we actually get to see each other? By the nature of my job, I worked mostly nights, while he obviously worked a regular day job. Plus, if I was going to pursue this music thing in earnest, there was practicing that would need to be done and gigs to secure. Not to mention the actual performances. I wanted to rush forward with my usual attitude of leaving those sorts of things for Future Hayden to work out, but Lucy mattered too much for me to just wing it. I didn't want us to fuck this up.

"So how public are we going with this thing? I mean, obviously, we aren't going to see other people, but are we telling anyone?"

He tossed his cup in a nearby trash can, and we paused on the sidewalk, turning to face each other. His car was just a few feet away, but I didn't want to get in until I was finished so I wouldn't drip my ice cream all over his car. He'd probably kill me.

"I'm basically an introvert, and I keep my personal life private at work, so I'm not sure how many people I'd be interested in telling, but I don't necessarily want to hide anything either. What about you?"

"I was thinking I'd update all my social media statuses to 'in a relationship,' and then maybe we could have a 'meet the boyfriend' party. It'd definitely have to be at your place because my apartment is too small. Though I've never seen your place. Is it big enough for a party of like thirty to forty people?"

His eyebrows had climbed up his forehead during my little speech and he was looking at me like I'd lost my damn mind. "Oh my god, your face!" I burst out laughing. "Relax, Lucy. I figured I'd tell my roommate, but I wasn't planning on making a big thing about it. I have quite a few friends here and there, but we aren't the type to call each other up and gossip about who's banging who. We're guys. It's whatever. I figure it'll come up organically in conversation when I get together with people. That alright with you?"

He visibly relaxed, his shoulders lowering from his ears. "Yes, of course. That's totally fine."

I chuckled at his attempt to play it cool and tossed the last of my soggy cone into the trash can, then licked my sticky fingers. Jonathan cringed but didn't comment, which I thought was a big step for him. I wiped my fingers with my napkin, then grabbed the front of his peacoat and pulled him toward me, placing a sticky kiss on his lips before pulling away.

He licked his lips. "Chocolate and raspberry. Good combo."

"I knew what I was doing. I'm an expert when it comes to ice cream flavor combinations." I grabbed his hand and tugged him toward his car. "Come on, *boyfriend,* let's go home so you can fuck me one more time before I leave."

I smirked as he tripped, then jogged to the car, beating me there.

I was pretty sure my rule-following, very much law-abiding boyfriend broke the speed limit the entire way home, getting us there in record time. I kept my hand high on his thigh the entire time, every so often brushing against his dick with my pinky, purely to torture him. With the way he kept shifting in his seat, I was pretty sure it was working.

When I'd asked him about sharing our relationship

status, I'd really wanted to know what we were telling our parents, but when he didn't bring them up in his response, I'd chickened out and let it drop rather than pressing further. I'd almost asked him on the car ride, but now that I'd spent the entire time teasing him, I'd gotten myself just as worked up and didn't want to ruin the mood.

I had my seatbelt off before he'd even put the car in Park and raced up the sidewalk, almost slipping on a patch of black ice but thankfully catching myself before I went down. "Watch out for ice," I called back as I wrestled with the door, trying to get it open. Why were doors so hard to open when you were in a hurry?

He made it up the stairs just as I pushed the door open, and I fell through the entrance with Lucy hot on my heels. We laughed as we raced to the bedroom, tearing off shoes and socks as we went. My foot got caught in my pants near the couch, and Lucy passed me by, pulling his sweater off as he crossed the threshold into the bedroom. The sound of his laughter, the pure joy in it, lit something up inside me. The transformation in him over the last couple of days filled me with gratitude that I got to be the one to bear witness to it. I hoped that our return to reality wouldn't diminish his light.

I finally freed my foot from my sweats and dropped them, along with my snowman underwear, right where I stood. My hat and hoodie were next, leaving me stark naked in the living room. I stalked toward the bedroom like a tiger on the hunt. "You better be ready for me in there, Lucy. 'Cause ready or not, here I come."

I expected a sarcastic retort but was instead met with a muffled grunt. I crossed the threshold of the bedroom and pulled up short, bursting into laughter at the sight in front of me. In his haste, Jonathan had tried to pull his button-down over his head without taking the time to undo all the buttons and was now stuck in a tangled mess. God, he was a sight with his jeans unbuttoned and riding low on his hips, his toned abs exposed and gleaming in the light from the window. It would have been hot as fuck if the man wasn't wriggling around, struggling to free himself of his shirt.

He abruptly stopped his struggle, giving a huff of frustration. I wanted to take pity on him and help him remove his shirt, but I couldn't resist the opportunity to tease him a little while he was in this helpless position.

I stepped forward and grabbed the zipper of his jeans, slowly lowering it and exposing his cotton-covered erection. Poor guy. It looked painful with the way it was trying to break free.

I drew his pants down over his hips, kneeling as I lowered the denim to the floor. I licked a stripe along the edge of the band of his briefs, eliciting a groan, and he began struggling with his bonds once again.

"Aw, Lucy. Have some patience."

"Goddamn it, Hay. Help me."

I mouthed the crown of his dick over the cotton. "I don't think so. I think I like you like this. Completely at my mercy."

I ran my hands up the backs of his legs to the curve of his ass. I took his globes in each of my hands, kneading the muscle, then grabbed the waistband of his briefs and yanked them down, letting them drop to the floor.

I tapped his ankle. "Step out of them, then spread your legs."

"What if I don't?" His tone was petulant. Damn, this was fun.

"Do you think negotiating is really a good play at this point? Pretty sure I have all the power here."

"I hate you," he said but stepped out of the underwear,

kicking them away from him and spreading his legs apart in a wide stance.

"That's a good boy." His cock twitched at my words, and I raised my eyebrows, even though he couldn't see me. "Do we have a bit of a praise kink, Luce? I could have some fun with that."

He growled, and my cock jumped in response. Apparently, I had a growly Jonathan kink.

I chuckled as I leaned forward, nosing into his groin, inhaling his scent. Once again, I brought my hands up to his ass, holding him in place. I continued moving my mouth around him, breathing him in but not yet taking him in fully. I was pretty sure the torture was killing him if the sounds coming from him were any indication. They were made up mostly of whimpers, with the occasional moan or growl mixed in. The sounds went straight to my own neglected cock, which was leaking like crazy.

Ignoring it, I brought my mouth to the underside of his balls, pulling one into my mouth and rolling it around my tongue. The musky, masculine scent of him, of my Lucy, was intoxicating as I switched from one ball to the other, lavishing it with the same attention as the first.

His hips bucked despite my hold on him, and he growled. "Hayden. Fucking do something. You're killing me."

"Good." I released his ass, grabbing the base of his cock with one hand and popping the fingers of the other into my mouth. "You ready?"

"Stop talking and get on with it."

I ran my wet finger up his crease, finding his hole and applying just the slightest bit of pressure. At his sharp intake of breath, I swallowed his cock all the way to the back of my throat in one swift motion and pressed my finger in to the first knuckle at the same time.

"Fuuuuuck."

I pulled back, running my tongue along the underside of his cock as I went, then swallowed him down all over again. The sounds coming from him were depraved, but his ass was clenched tight, not allowing me in any farther.

I pulled off him again, employing suction as I moved, then released him with a pop. "You gonna let me in, Luce?" I wiggled my finger, trying to encourage him to relax and open up for me.

"Not without lube. And please let me out of this goddamned shirt. My hands are going numb." His words were desperate, and I took pity on him.

I stood and undid the buttons, releasing him from his shirt. Finally free, he pounced, flipping us and tackling me to the bed. "You're going to pay for that."

I laughed as he climbed up my body, grabbing my hands and pinning them above my head. "Promise?" I wiggled my eyebrows.

"Fucker." He dove in, kissing me until we were both breathless, rutting against each other, dicks leaking between us. He released my hands, sitting up to rummage in the drawer, finally coming up with a condom and lube.

He tossed the lube at me. Unprepared, it bounced off my chest and rolled off, and I scrambled to find it on the bed next to me. In the meantime, he grabbed my dick and began rolling the condom on.

Baffled, I raised my eyebrows in question.

"I want you to fuck me, Hay."

"What? I don't need that with you, Luce. I know it makes you uncomfortable."

"Maybe it has in the past. But I want to try it, at least once, and if there's anyone I would trust to top me, it's you."

My stomach flip-flopped. I was honored he would trust me with this but terrified I'd hurt him.

"Are you sure?"

He took the lube from me, poured some over my condom-covered cock, then on his fingers before he reached behind himself and began to awkwardly try to work himself open. I took the little bottle from him, lubed my own fingers, and grabbed his arm, stopping him. "Let me."

I pulled him forward so he was straddling my abdomen, making it easier to reach. With one hand, I stroked his cock and his eyes closed on a full-body shudder. With the other hand, I slid back to his hole, circling it with my lubed fingertip and pressing it inside. I got farther in than last time, but now I moved slower, pressing deeper, looking for that spot I knew would light him up.

"Relax for me, Lucy."

"I'm trying."

"Honey, we don't have to do this."

His eyes flew open. "I want to try."

"I know, but you have to relax. I don't want to hurt you." He looked so frustrated. "Let's switch places. I think it'll be easier for you if you don't have to hold yourself up."

He climbed off me, and we switched places. "Pull up your knees. Let me see that pretty hole." He did as I asked, spreading his legs wide, his pucker on display for me. I leaned forward and kissed him, pressing my finger past his ring of muscle once again as I took his mouth in mine. With my other hand, I stroked his dick, and the distraction worked as I slowly felt him relax, and I was able to slip my finger in a little farther. I continued to work him, both his dick and his hole, adding one finger at a time until I had three fingers buried deep. I found the spongy button inside him and tapped, gratified when his hips punched up and he let out a string of curses as he writhed on my fingers.

"That's it, Lucy. Go a little crazy for me."

I continued to stroke him as I stretched him, alternating scissoring my fingers with tapping on his prostate until he was a begging, whimpering mess. Satisfied he was sufficiently prepped, I withdrew my fingers, marveling at the sight of his hole so open and ready for me. I placed my cockhead at his entrance and pressed forward ever so slightly, wanting desperately to bury myself inside of him but wanting to be sure one more time this was what he wanted.

"You sure? Last chance to back out."

"Fucking fuck me already."

My cock jumped at those words, at the needy demand in them. Had anyone ever wanted me this much? I sure as shit didn't think I'd ever wanted anyone as much as I wanted him in that moment.

I pressed my dick forward, breaching his entrance, taking my time to ensure I didn't hurt him, despite the fact I desperately wanted to bury myself to the hilt and pound him into next week.

Halfway in, he took matters into his own hands, wrapping his legs around me and using those powerful runner's legs to pull me the rest of the way into him. I slid home and took a moment to let him adjust. If I was being honest, I needed a moment myself. His eyes were locked on mine, the blue pools so intense it was hard to look at him, yet I couldn't tear my eyes away. What was this between us? It was unlike anything I'd ever experienced.

He tilted his hips ever so slightly, encouraging me to move and sending electric currents through my cock. I was so close to losing it already, buried in the heat of him, so tight and warm. I thought I might burn alive.

I pulled back and slid home again, undulating my hips as I began to set a moderate rhythm. "Faster, Hayden. You aren't going to break me."

"You topping from the bottom?"

"Damn right. Would you expect anything less?"

My face lit in a wide grin. "Not from my Lucy."

I started to pick up the pace, delicious sparks moving through me with each thrust. He took his dick in hand, stroking in time with each punch of my hips. "Faster, Hay. Fucking wreck me."

"Shit." I pounded into him, hard and fast, over and over again, grunting and panting with each stroke. He closed his eyes, a little wrinkle forming on his brow as he continued to stroke himself faster and faster.

His fist was a blur, and I thought he was close, but I was also fairly sure I hadn't pegged his prostate yet, and if this was his first time bottoming, I was going to motherfucking make sure I did it right. I pulled his legs off my waist, pushing his knees back to his shoulders, changing the angle and rocking my hips up into him. Something between a shriek and a groan ripped from his lips, and his dick erupted, unloading rope after rope of thick cum all over his chest. I let loose my own roar as I buried myself deep inside him and unloaded into the condom. Time seemed to stand still as I came in never-ending pulses.

As I came back to myself, he reached for me, pulling me forward on top of him, holding me against his chest, our sweat and his cum trapped between us. I lay like that for a long time, listening to his heartbeat as it tried to return to a normal tempo.

"Holy shit. That was...wow," he said between breaths.

I tilted my head up to look at him. "It was good?"

"Yeah, Hay. It was damn good."

"Thank fuck."

The grin he shot my way could have lit up half the county, and I'd never been happier.

21

JONATHAN

December 27

Morning brought with it a sense of impending doom. As if sensing our mood, thick clouds had rolled in, hanging heavy and blocking out the sun. A part of me hoped for another snowstorm, an excuse to hide away just a little longer, but I knew we needed to get back to reality eventuality. Better to know now if this thing between us could withstand the stresses of the real world.

But damn, I wanted to put it off just a little longer.

We took a leisurely shower, soaping each other up and jacking each other off until we were painting each other's bellies with our cum while the water ran cold. Packing didn't take long, so before we knew it, we were standing outside his car, and I was trying to figure out what to say. How did I tell Hayden that he'd fundamentally changed the course of my life in just a few days? That was crazy, right?

But I knew it was the truth. Even if things didn't work out between us in the long-term, I knew the trajectory of my life would be forever changed. Hayden had shown me that people weren't always who they appeared to be on the surface. That snap judgments said more about the observer than the person being judged. And the fact that I'd almost missed out on the opportunity to truly get to know him, simply because I'd been so sure my worldview was the only one that was acceptable, made me wonder what else—who else—I'd been closed off to.

He'd taught me to laugh.

And I thought, maybe, he'd shown me what it felt like to fall in love.

I pressed my forehead to his, eyes closed, breathing him in as if I could somehow grab his essence and wrap myself in it, even after he was gone.

Good God, he'd turned me into a sap.

"I'm gonna miss you." His voice was almost a whisper.

I smiled. Maybe I wasn't the only sap here.

"It's not goodbye forever. I'll be back in the city later tonight. I just have to clean up the cabin and lock everything up." I nuzzled his nose. "You want to come to my place after your shift?"

"No, that's okay. I'll be at work pretty late and you have to be up early." I could hear the pout in his voice, even with my eyes closed. A part of me was disappointed, but his reasoning made sense. It was sensible. "With you working during the day and most of my shifts being at night, it already feels like we're never going to see each other."

I tipped his chin up, forcing him to look at me. He'd shaved this morning, his boss preferring the clean-shaven look for his servers, and I missed the feel of stubble against my fingers. "We'll work it out. I'll come sit in your section, and you can take me out to lunch, and we'll find other moments in between. And maybe it doesn't work tonight, but there will be other nights...nights I can have my way with you." I waggled my eyebrows comically, something I didn't think I'd ever done in my life, but I wanted to make him smile. I was rewarded with a small chuckle. "I'm in this with you. I mean it, Hay. I'm willing to work for it. You're worth it."

He launched himself at me, wrapping his arms around me in a bear hug. I didn't think anyone had ever squeezed me so tight. "I'm so glad your wife divorced you, and you ended up here drinking away your holiday."

I barked out a laugh. God, he was ridiculous. "I'm glad you got in a fight with your dad and ran away to the cabin and got snowed in with me."

We held each other for a long moment before he finally pulled away. "I better get going. If I don't rip off the Band-Aid, I'm never going to leave."

I pressed a quick kiss to his lips but pulled away before it could get out of hand. He opened the car door and slipped into the driver's seat, shutting the door behind him. Hayden looked like he was trying to decide whether to reopen the door and say something, but he must have decided against it because he gave me a small wave and then backed out of the driveway. Before I knew it, his car was fading away in the distance.

The cabin felt cold and empty without him as if he'd taken all of his warmth with him. I wandered aimlessly, trying to decide what to do with myself. I walked back to the bedroom and stripped the bed, throwing a load of linens and towels into the washing machine. Next, I moved into the kitchen, going through cabinets and packing the food that could be taken back and tossing the stuff that wasn't worth keeping.

By late afternoon, I stood in the empty cabin, taking final inventory in preparation for loading my car. I'd finished the laundry, cleaned out the fridge, and the entire place smelled like lemon and bleach. I walked back into the bedroom, tucked my phone charger into my duffel, and took one last look around.

Hayden had given life to this cabin, filling it with laughter, music, and his own brand of relentless energy, in a way it hadn't seen since Grandpa Sam had been alive. God, Grandpa would have loved Hayden. The two of them would have been thick as thieves.

Shaking my head at the way I was mooning over my boyfriend like a lovesick teenager, I hefted my duffel onto my shoulder and moved into the living room, turning off the light behind me. It was as I was putting on my coat that I spotted it. Hayden's guitar was resting against the wall right by the door. It had been partially hidden by my coat so I hadn't noticed it.

It felt like a sign. With our conflicting schedules, we'd decided we'd go to our separate houses in the city tonight, but that felt a little bit like cutting off my nose to spite my face. I wanted to see him, didn't I? I was a grown-ass adult and if I wanted to stay up late to see my boyfriend, who was going to stop me?

I picked up the guitar and my duffel and headed out to my car, making sure to secure the cabin behind me. I'd just take the guitar over to Hayden's and wait for him to get off work. Worst case, he'd take the guitar, and I'd head home. Best case, he'd let me stay.

Either way, I'd get to see him tonight.

22

HAYDEN

It had been a long fucking day. The drive back to the city had been uneventful. However, I'd spent most of it with my thoughts jumping all over the place between worrying about whether Jonathan and I could really maintain a relationship in the city, how I was going to tell my father about my desire to pursue music, wondering what the specials would be at Olive & Vine tonight, debating how we were going to tell our parents we were seeing each other, and wondering how the proposal went with my roommate.

Thankfully, my shift at Olive & Vine had been a busy one. The week between Christmas and New Year's was always crazy in the service industry, even on a Monday. People were tired of cooking for their families and often came into the restaurant to take a night off from cooking. It had been a great distraction from all the worry, and I'd made some great tips, but now, as I pulled into the parking lot of my apartment complex, it hit me that after sleeping in Jonathan's bed for the last three nights, I'd be sleeping alone tonight. It was a depressing thought.

I pulled into an open spot, killed the engine, and started across the lot toward the entrance to my building. I was nearly past it when I spotted a car that looked an awful lot like Jonathan's. We didn't see a lot of black Audis in this lot. It was more of a ten-year-old Corolla sort of building. I slowed my steps and approached the car cautiously, just in case it wasn't Lucy's.

Bless. He was asleep in the driver's seat.

I knocked on the window gently, but it still managed to scare the bejeezus out of him. He startled, his head snapping up and his arms flailing, one of them hitting the steering wheel. I stepped back so he could open the car door and get out.

"What are you doing here?"

My heart was racing with anticipation and nerves. I was thrilled to see him, but there was a part of me that wondered if he was here because he'd changed his mind and wanted to break it off before we got carried away. Would I always be consumed with this doubt?

He turned and opened the door to the backseat, and pulled out my guitar. "You forgot this."

"You came over tonight just to bring me my guitar?"

"No."

"No?"

Lips curved in a small smile, he stepped closer, cupping my cheek and rubbing my chin with his thumb. "The guitar was an excuse to do this." He leaned in and kissed me sweetly. Tenderly.

Lovingly.

He pulled back, leaving me in a daze. "Don't you have to work tomorrow?" I asked, still in disbelief that he was actually here.

"Yeah, but I wanted to see you. I didn't want to wait." He

shrugged and offered me a rueful smile. "Is it okay that I came over tonight?" He looked a little unsure, which somehow made me feel like we were on even ground. Maybe I wasn't the only one feeling insecure about this whole thing.

"It's more than okay. I'm so glad you're here." I threw my arms around him in a hug, and he melted into me as if he was relieved.

I pulled back when he shivered, and that's when I noticed he wasn't wearing a coat. "Where's your coat?"

"I took it off on the drive. The car was warm."

"How long have you been sitting out here?"

He pulled up his wrist and looked at his smartwatch. "A couple of hours. I didn't know which apartment was yours, and I didn't know if your roommate was home."

"He probably is. But you could have just texted me. I would have come over to your house."

He leaned in, crowding into my space, his lips so close I could feel his breath. "Maybe I liked the idea of being here when you got home."

My heart melted into a puddle of goo and slid all the way into my feet as he leaned in and kissed me, leisurely twining his tongue with mine and erasing some of the doubts that kept creeping in, no matter how hard I tried to keep them at bay.

Despite the heat of our embrace, he gave another full-bodied shiver, and I pulled back. "You want to come up?"

"And meet your roommate?"

"Sure. But mostly, I was hoping I could talk you into fucking me."

"*Jesus.*" I felt his dick twitch against my hip, and I grinned "Wait. While he's in the next room?"

I chuckled, taking the guitar from him and turning

toward the entrance, tugging him behind me. "I've heard him fucking his fiancée at all hours. Neither of them is quiet about it. It'll be fine."

We'd only made it a few steps when he dug his heels in and pulled to a stop. I turned to look at him. "I don't know if I can...*perform* with people in the next room." The crease between his brows was adorable.

"Ah. A challenge. I like a challenge."

I tugged his hand again, dragging him up the stairs to my third-floor apartment. I pushed through the door, immediately spotting my roommate and his fiancée cuddled up on the couch.

"Hey, guys. This is my boyfriend, Jonathan." I gestured toward the couch. "This is Sean and Frannie." All parties gave an awkward wave, eyes wide as they took stock of each other. "We're going to go fuck now," I said as I tugged a groaning Lucy down the hall toward my room at the back of the apartment.

"Hey, isn't he your...?" Sean called out.

"Yep," I said, without turning back. We crossed into my room, and I set my guitar down, then shut the door, pushing him against it.

I plastered myself to him, shoving my knee between his legs and pressing my cock against his hip, grinding against him obscenely. I pushed my hand up his shirt, wanting to feel his skin. "Damn, Lucy. Your skin is so cold." I added my other hand, pushing up his sweater so I could feel him with both hands. He obliged me by removing the sweater completely, and I took advantage, diving in to run the flat of my tongue across one pebbled nipple. He moaned, yanking at my hair as I nipped and sucked at him.

Abruptly, he yanked my head back, shoving me away from him. "On the bed."

Oh. Fuck.

"It's like that, huh? I like it when bossy Jonathan comes out to play."

"Don't make me repeat myself." He shoved me back another step, fire in his eyes. "And I told you to call me Lucy."

Goddamn. I stepped back, tripping over a pair of shoes and nearly landing hard on my ass. I started to take off my pants, but his voice stopped me. "I didn't tell you to strip. Just get on the bed."

My cock was painfully hard, straining against the fly of my work pants, but I did as he asked, lying on my back, watching as he stalked toward me like a tiger on the prowl. He stepped over the pair of shoes I'd nearly tripped on, stopping when his legs met the edge of the bed. I squirmed under the intensity of his gaze, wondering what he was going to do next.

Whatever it was, I was here for it. This bossy take-no-shit side of him was hot as fuck.

He bent over and removed my shoes, untying each one slowly before removing them. My socks followed next, and then he leaned over the bed, unbuttoned my pants, and slowly lowered my zipper.

He continued in this manner, moving methodically and without haste, never saying a word. It took every bit of my self-control not to speak—part of me wanted to flip him some shit, just to see what he'd do—but I also wanted to see how it would play out if I gave him complete control.

He leaned forward and buried his nose in my groin, nuzzling the juncture of my thigh and my sack. The feel of his scruff—more a beard at this point—rubbing against the skin of my inner thigh had me arching my neck, a strangled groan wrenched from my lips.

He eased my pants down, his tongue following a path from my waistband to my ankles, sending goosebumps skittering across my bare skin. I wiggled and squirmed, my entire existence narrowed to his assault on my senses.

He tapped my thigh. "Flip over."

My eyes popped open—I hadn't even realized they were shut. "What?"

"Flip over. On your belly."

My eyes widened, but I hastened to comply, flipping myself onto my stomach. I heard the sound of a zipper, followed by the sound of something—I was hoping his jeans—dropping to the floor. I only had a moment to register the feel of his breath on the back of my thigh before he sank his teeth into my ass, biting hard enough through the fabric of my red-and-green plaid briefs that I was fairly sure there'd be a mark tomorrow. I fucking loved it. Loved the idea of him marking me.

"God, I love this ass." He bit the other cheek, and I pushed back into his face in reflex. He snagged a finger under my waistband and pulled, drawing the fabric below the curve.

"Hips up, ass in the air," he said, pulling my underwear down, my cock springing free beneath me. A string of precum stretched from the tip of my aching dick to the fabric of my bedspread as I got on all fours with my ass in the air.

Despite my resolve to let him have control, I quipped, "So much for being unable to perform." I'd never been very good at controlling my mouth, and I paid for it when a loud crack echoed in the room, his hand connecting with my flesh. My cock jumped in response, even as I bit down on my pillow to keep from crying out. His tongue replaced the spot he'd just smacked, soothing the sting yet somehow sending my lust skyrocketing. I transferred my weight to one hand so I could stroke my aching cock with the other, but Jonathan wasn't having it. He batted my hand away, yanking it back down to the bed.

"Not yet."

"C'mon, Lucy," I whined. "I'm dying."

"Payback's a bitch."

I groaned as I realized this was retaliation for not freeing him from his shirt last night. The bastard was going to torture me three times worse than I'd tortured him.

Two hands spread my cheeks, and before I could register what was happening, I felt his tongue slipping along my crease. I froze, my brain scrambling as I tried to make sense of what was happening. Jonathan had been horrified at the mere thought of me eating him out just a few days ago. He couldn't possibly be returning the favor.

And yet...

His tongue brushed across my hole, and every muscle in my body clenched at the shock.

"C'mon, Hay. Let me in."

I let out a breath, forcing myself to relax. I loved being eaten out, and if Lucy was game to try it, who was I to stop him? He licked another stripe down my crease, this time applying more pressure, moving with purpose. I moaned into the pillow, trying to keep from crying out as he licked and bit at me. Then he was pressing his tongue into me, probing my entrance with short jabs, sending ripples of pleasure through my body. I tried to hold still, but I couldn't stop myself from wiggling as he licked and sucked my hole.

"Luce... Please..." I wasn't even sure what I was begging for at this point. My dick was angry at being ignored and leaking all over the place, my balls were aching, and my hole was being assaulted. But it wasn't enough. I wanted to be filled. Taken. Used.

Jonathan climbed on the bed behind me, draping himself over me and speaking softly into my ear. I sill had my shirt on, so the contact wasn't direct skin-to-skin, but I sighed with pleasure at the feel of him wrapped around me. It was like being covered with a weighted blanket. Only the blanket smelled like Jonathan and had a dick that was poking me in the ass. "Where's your lube?"

"In the drawer." I nodded my head to the right toward my bedside table. He rummaged around for a moment—was my dildo still in there?—before I heard the drawer shut and the telltale snick of the lid popping open.

Cool liquid trickled down my crack, and I hissed in response. He began slowly stretching me with one finger, then two, eventually working up to three. I heard him rip open a condom, and I tried once again to relieve my aching cock while he prepped himself, but he smacked my hand away, growling, "What did I tell you?"

I whimpered, but just when I thought I was going to lose my mind, I felt him nudge my opening, pushing into me in one fluid stroke. Fully seated, his hips pressed against me, he began to rock in short, undulating strokes, each one pulling a little whimper from me as if he were dismantling me one piece at a time.

Finally, he reached around and grabbed my neglected dick, and I nearly wept at the contact. He began to stroke me harder, thrusting into me faster and faster, pegging my prostate with each stroke, lighting up my entire body like the Fourth of July.

"Harder," I gritted out, desperately chasing my orgasm. "I want to be able to feel you three days from now."

He growled and kicked into another gear, jackhammering into me like a man possessed. The headboard hit the wall, something tipped over on my nightstand, and I buried my face in my pillow, screaming as my orgasm ripped through me like a freight train.

Over and over again, my dick pulsed onto the bed below as Lucy continued to pound me into oblivion until he let go of my nearly spent dick, instead grabbing my hips and pulling me into him as he buried himself to the hilt on a mighty yell. I felt him throb inside me, his fingers bruising my skin where he gripped me while he filled the condom.

Moments later, he collapsed on top of me, and my arms gave out, my muscles liquefied after holding myself up for so long.

As I floated back to earth, I felt his breath against my ear as he asked, "You okay?"

"Hell. Yes."

"I wasn't too rough?" Ah, there was my sweet, concerned Lucy, replacing bossy, growly Jonathan.

I tried to turn my head to look at him, but it was too difficult at this angle, so I mustered up the strength to shove him off me and rolled over. Gone was the assertive, demanding man who'd fucked me. In his place was my sweet boyfriend, worry and doubt etched into his features as he looked down at me.

I reached up and brushed the side of his cheek, curling my hand around the back of his neck. "I like it rough. I like it slow. I like it fast. I like it however you want it."

He searched my eyes as if trying to verify my honesty. I pulled him down and kissed him sweetly. "I promise I'll tell you if there's ever something I don't like. Okay?"

Accepting my answer, he nodded, his features relaxing. He removed the condom, tying it off and tossing it in the trash in the corner before, flipping off the light, and climbing back into bed. I removed my shirt, then invited him under the covers with me, where he curled up beside me, his head on my shoulder.

I savored the feel of him tucked into my side, running my fingertips up and down his back. Most of the time, it was he who held me, so this was nice for a change. Especially after he'd been so dominant just moments ago. As much as I'd liked that little bit of role play, this felt like balance was restored.

"Lucy?"

"Mmm?" His voice was hazy like he was almost asleep.

"I'm glad you came here tonight."

He snuggled in, draping his arm over my middle. "Mmm. Me too."

23

JONATHAN

December 28

"Jonathan? Hello?"

My eyes flicked up to the man standing in my doorway. My coworker, Louis, was looking at me, eyebrows raised in question. I wondered how long he'd been trying to get my attention.

"Sorry. What's up?"

He took that as an invitation to walk into my office and sit in one of the chairs in front of my desk. I frowned.

"Relax, Jon-o. You look like you ate a lemon." Louis had a habit of giving everyone bad nicknames and inviting himself into your business. We'd worked together for years, and his work was impeccable, but his habit of poking around, trying to open me up, was annoying. I much preferred to keep my professional and personal lives separate.

"What did you need, Louis?"

"How was your trip out to the cabin?" He leaned back in

the chair, crossing an ankle over his knee, making himself comfortable.

I raised a brow. "How did you know I went to the cabin?" As far as I could recall, I hadn't told anyone where I was going. I'd marked myself *out of the office* on my calendar and walked out on the twenty-second.

He shrugged as if it wasn't a big deal that he was in my personal business. "I just assumed with your divorce being finalized last week, you'd want to get away for a bit."

"How did you know— You know what? That doesn't matter. What can I help you with, Louis?"

"Oh, I just, uh, I just wanted to chat."

"We don't *chat*, Louis. If there's nothing you *need*, I have work to do." I turned toward my computer, effectively dismissing him.

He stood in a huff, and I thought I heard him mutter "Dick" under his breath as he walked out, but I couldn't be sure.

The fact was, he was right. I was being a dick, especially considering I'd had more sex in the last week than I'd had in at least a year. But what had started as a rough morning had turned into a truly shitty day when I got a text from my father around lunchtime. One that was almost immediately followed by a text from Hayden.

It would appear we were being summoned to dinner. Suzanne and my father were home from their trip and were inviting us to a belated Christmas dinner on the thirtieth, two days from now. I was sure this was Suzanne's doing, as my father had never been sentimental about such things and would have likely preferred to let the holiday come and go without fanfare.

I opened the messages on my phone, rereading each one that had come through.

DAD

We are having Christmas dinner on
Thursday. You are expected to be there.
6:30 sharp

As if I had ever been late for anything in my life.

I hadn't responded to his text. No response was necessary. It was expected that I would be there, and any plans I might already have were to be canceled or rescheduled.

I flipped over to the other text I'd received. It had been three texts, actually, coming in rapid-fire, one after the next.

HAYDEN

Did you get a summons for dinner on
Thursday?

I have to work, but I can probably get out
of it.

What are we telling our parents about us?

This one *did* require a response, but I hadn't formulated one yet. This thing with Hayden was so new. My relationship with him felt sweet and tender and...fragile. Not because our connection was weak, but like all new living things, it needed nurture and care. I wanted more time for us to get our bearings, to find sturdy footing, before we exposed our relationship to the scrutiny of our family. Of my father.

But I didn't want to hide him either. The stepbrother thing and the age gap didn't bother me anymore. Those things didn't matter. Against all odds, and despite our differences, he was my person. None of the rest mattered.

But that was easier said than done. I could say it didn't matter what my father thought about any of this, but old habits died hard. I'd spent the whole of my life seeking his approval. I couldn't just shut that off, no matter how much I wanted to.

Then there was Hayden. I knew he and his mom were close. I didn't want to be the source of any sort of conflict between them. He already struggled with his relationship with his dad. I didn't want him to be at odds with both of his parents.

As I was contemplating all of this, another text came through, startling me when my phone vibrated in my hand.

HAYDEN

Are you still mad?

I let out a breath, scrubbing my hand over my face, guilt snaking its way through me. I'd been such a dick when I'd left this morning, and none of it had been his fault. Factor that in with the fact that I hadn't responded to his texts about the dinner with our parents, and he'd likely worked himself up into a ball of worry.

Noting the time was nearing three o'clock, I shut off my computer and shrugged on my coat. With half the office on vacation during this holiday week, I'd been looking forward to catching up on some work while it was quiet, but it was evident I wasn't going to get anything done today.

I strode out of my office and headed toward the elevator, my long legs eating up the carpet as I moved with purpose.

"Where're you going, Jon-O?"

The elevator doors opened, and I punched the button for the parking garage. "To see my boyfriend," I called out as the doors were closing, enjoying the look of surprise on Louis's face. I'd probably pay for that impulsive comment later, but right now, I had more important things on my mind.

❄

I texted Hayden on the way down to my car, asking him to meet me at The Daily Grind, a coffee shop about a block away from Olive & Vine. We were only going to have about an hour to talk before he needed to be at work, but I knew this was a conversation worth having in person.

He hadn't deserved the way I'd treated him this morning, and I owed him an apology. He had me so off-kilter and out of my routine, and while I'd enjoyed exploring the freedom that came with just rolling with it back at the cabin, I'd not handled it well back here in the real world.

It had started with me oversleeping this morning, having not set an alarm last night before passing out in a post-orgasmic coma. I hadn't planned on spending the night when I'd shown up at Hayden's last night. Hell, I hadn't even stopped at my own home and unpacked first. I'd just shown up wanting to see him. To fill my senses with him. Holding him, breathing him in, gazing into his deep brown eyes had been the only things on my mind. I hadn't thought I'd fuck him. I certainly hadn't planned to spend the night.

I'd found myself waking up this morning two hours later than usual, with sunlight streaming in rather than the darkness that came with a December predawn morning. Hayden had still been asleep when I'd thrown off the covers, bolting out of bed, naked as the day I was born. I'd stumbled over a pair of shoes and a stack of books, but it had been the pair of jeans that had done me in. I'd gotten my feet tangled in them and fallen hard, catching my shoulder on the corner of his dresser, eliciting a shout that had finally woken him up.

Apparently, I'd also woken his roommate, who'd banged

on the wall and yelled, "You guys okay in there?" which had only frustrated and embarrassed me further. Angry, I'd turned my frustration on Hayden, who'd been sitting gloriously naked in the center of the bed, eyes wide as he took in my appearance.

He'd come up on his knees, scooching himself to the end of the bed. "Are you okay?"

"No, I'm not fucking okay. Goddammit, Hayden. Your room is a fucking disaster." I'd rubbed my bruised shoulder, then reached for my pants, yanking them on with angry, disjointed movements. "I have to go. I'm late."

I'd at least had the presence of mind to kiss him on the forehead once I was fully dressed, I recalled. I might have been frustrated, and my shoulder had been on fire, but I was still in love with the human tornado.

I stopped in my tracks three steps from opening the door to the entrance of the coffee shop. Someone came out, nearly running into me as I stood directly in the path of anyone entering or exiting the place. Still, I didn't budge from the spot.

I was in love with Hayden.

How was that possible? It hadn't even been a week. I'd had some thoughts about it yesterday, but I'd attributed that to my sappy feelings about him leaving the cabin. I'd thought I was *on the way* to falling in love. I couldn't already be there. Could I?

I mentally shook myself and entered the coffee shop. These were all thoughts I could work through later. Things I needed to examine further with proper diligence and adequate time.

I spotted Hayden in the back corner and started making my way toward him, bypassing the line for coffee. I didn't want to waste time standing in line when I had things I needed to say.

As it turned out, Hayden had already bought me a coffee. He slid it toward me as I took my seat across from him, noting that his smile was forced and he wouldn't quite meet my eyes.

I sipped my coffee, mostly because it was there, not really tasting it beyond noting that it was black, as I liked it. Absently, I took his hand in mine as I faced him, trying to organize my thoughts. My revelation on the sidewalk was making it difficult for me to remember why I'd called him here in the first place.

He stared at our clasped hands for a moment before reluctantly drawing his eyes up to mine. The worry in his expression nearly broke my heart. I hated that I'd been the one to put that there.

"Hay, I'm—"

"I cleaned my—"

We had spoken at the same time and chuckled nervously in response.

"Go ahead," I said, sipping my coffee to indicate he should speak first.

"Oh, I was just going to tell you I cleaned my room today."

My breath left me in a whoosh. While I valued a clean space, I could read between the lines here and see Hayden hadn't done it out of any desire to tidy his room but rather because he was afraid I was going to be upset with him. It was the way I'd lived my entire life. Doing things in the hope they'd be pleasing to my father, or at the very least, that I wouldn't upset him. And here we were, with Hayden doing the same thing. I really was just like my father.

"Hay, you didn't have to do that."

"I know you like a clean space. It's not a big deal."

"Well, yes, I do, but I don't want you to do things like that because you're worried I'm mad at you. I shouldn't have yelled at you like I did. I was angry that I'd failed to set an alarm and was going to be late, and I took it out on you. It really wasn't about the messy room, and I shouldn't have spoken to you like that."

"It's okay. My room *was* a mess. And I knew you weren't really upset with *me*, but it felt good to do something about it anyway."

"I just..." I leaned forward, pulling my hand from his so I could cup his face instead, "I don't want you to be afraid of disappointing me. Not like I was with my father. There will likely be things we'll have to adjust to between the two of us, but I don't ever want you to think you're a disappointment."

"You're projecting, Luce. It's really not a big deal." He turned his face, pressing his lips to the center of my palm. "And speaking of your father, what are we going to tell them when we go over for dinner?"

I wasn't convinced he was being entirely truthful about his feelings on the matter or his motivations for cleaning his room, but I let it drop and vowed to do better in the future. I never wanted him to doubt that he was lo—cared for.

There was that damn L-word again.

I took his hand in mine once again. "What would you like to tell them?"

"I'm kind of all over the place on it. I want the whole world to know you're mine, but I also kind of want to keep us in a bubble for a little while longer. It's all so new, and we're still figuring things out, and I don't want anyone else's judgment to cast a shadow over this. You know?"

I did know. I'd had similar thoughts on my way over here. And yet, I didn't like hearing him voice those thoughts aloud. It made me wonder if he had doubts about us. About me.

"So you don't want to tell them?"

"I mean, kind of?" He said it like a question, like he wasn't sure what my reaction would be. Something churned in my gut. It didn't feel right. But I also wanted to respect his wishes. Especially after I'd been such a dick to him this morning.

"We can wait if you want to. Or at least we can try. It'll be hard to keep my hands off you."

"Ooh! Maybe we should meet up and fuck before we go over there. Get it out of our system."

"Jesus, Hay." I shook my head, exasperated at his antics but also pleased to see the return of his sense of humor. I never wanted to diminish his light.

He waggled his eyebrows at me. "You want to meet at my place or yours?"

I couldn't do anything but grin at him. Damn, if he wasn't good for my soul. "How about we start with you coming over to my house after work tonight." I reached across and pulled him toward me. "I'll show you how sorry I am for the way I behaved this morning," I said against his lips.

"In that case, I take it back. I'm very angry at you. You'll have to spend hours making it up to me."

I chuckled as I took his lips with mine, teasing his tongue for just a moment before pulling back. "You should probably get going if you don't want to be late."

He looked at his phone, then shot out of his chair, hastily pulling on his coat. I walked him out to his car but stopped him before he got in. "I really am sorry about this morning. Please don't accept that behavior from me. You deserve better."

"It's alright. I—" He let out a burst of air. "You know what? You're right. I do." He pressed a sweet kiss to my lips. "Thank you."

24

HAYDEN

December 30

"You gonna ring the doorbell?"

"Are you?" Jonathan raised his eyebrows in challenge.

"I mean, what if we just skip this whole thing? You could just do dinner without me, right? I like that plan. Thanks for taking one for the team." I bro-slapped him on the shoulder and made like I was going to head down the steps.

"I don't think so, you little shit." Jonathan grabbed my arm and pulled me back until we were standing chest to chest, one of my legs between his, with his arms wrapped around me. "We agreed we weren't going to tell them about us. Why are you so nervous?"

"I don't know. Do you really think we can hide this? I feel like I have hearts in my eyes, and it's going to be really obvious." Since Lucy'd apologized for the way he'd snapped at me, we'd had a really good couple of days. I'd stayed at his house the last two nights, and we'd even had a lunch date today. I'd surprised him when I'd stopped by his office to take him out for sushi. The office had been quiet, but some guy named Louis had appeared out of nowhere while we waited for the elevator. Jonathan had practically shoved me into the elevator before I could introduce myself.

Tonight, we'd arrived separately at our parents' house, figuring it'd look weird if we arrived together, considering that in the past, we'd barely spoken more than just to make polite conversation. But now, as I stood on the porch, wrapped in his arms, I was starting to realize just how hard it would be to keep this thing between us a secret. I was too far gone for him to hide it.

"I guess I'm just having second thoughts about—"

We jumped apart at the last second, just as the door opened. My mom stood in the doorway, darting a glance between us, obviously wondering why we were standing out there without ringing the doorbell.

"Were you guys going to come in or just stand out in the cold all night?"

"Hi, Mom!" I leaned forward and kissed her on the cheek. "We just happened to arrive at the same time, and you caught us right as we were about to ring the bell."

"Well, come on in. It's cold out there!"

I glanced back at Jonathan as I crossed over the threshold. He looked stricken, and I realized I hadn't finished my sentence. I tried to turn back to explain I wasn't having second thoughts about *us* but rather about keeping it a secret. Too late, Mom was dragging me down the hallway toward the kitchen. I'd just have to try to get him alone to clear it up.

We entered the kitchen, which they'd just had remodeled a couple of months ago. She'd chosen light and airy colors with a white countertop and gray cabinets. But the thing I'd been drooling over was the stove. It was a beautiful six-burner gas range with a dual convection oven. I was dying to cook something on it.

Jonathan came in behind me, looking rather subdued. I wanted desperately to pull him aside to talk to him and clarify what I'd been about to say, but I wasn't sure how to do so without drawing attention to us, and I didn't want to give anything away about our relationship unless he was on board.

Mom poured us each a glass of wine, asked us how our holiday was, and then proceeded to launch into a story about her trip. It wasn't that she was selfish, so much as that she was excitable. And in this instance, it was fortunate because that meant Jonathan and I didn't have to lie or skirt around the truth of our own holiday adventures.

When the timer went off for the oven, she shooed us into the dining room while she put the finishing touches on dinner. I'd offered to help, but she'd refused, so Jonathan and I moved into the next room.

"Hey." I put my hand on his arm, stopping him from pulling his chair out. He peered at me, his face a mask of cold indifference that had my heart freezing in my chest. "I didn't mean to say that I was having second—" Jon came into the room, cutting me off once again, and I pulled my arm back, moving around to the other side to sit opposite of Lucy.

Mom came in with a platter loaded with pot roast, having opted against the traditional fare since it was just the four of us. It dawned on me that this was one of only a handful of times when it had been just the four of us gathering for a meal. Mom had come from a large family, so holiday meals often consisted of a larger group with aunts, uncles, and cousins in attendance. Tonight, we wouldn't have extended family as a buffer. Well, with Lucy misunderstanding what I had been about to say earlier, perhaps it wouldn't be so hard to pretend we were no more than acquaintances.

"So, Jonathan, what did you do for the holiday?" Mom asked as she passed him the serving platter. She must have forgotten she'd already asked us in the kitchen.

"I spent a few days up at the cabin."

"Oh? By yourself?" Bless my mom. She looked so affronted by that idea.

Jon spoke up from the end of the table. "Who else would he have gone up there with when his divorce was just finalized?"

"Thanks, Dad." Jonathan's tone was dry, but those little digs from his father were just the type of thing that I knew got under his skin. I nudged the side of his calf with my toe, hoping to remind him he wasn't alone, but he pulled his legs back out of my reach without looking at me.

"Well, honey, what about you? What have you been up to? How was Christmas with your dad's family?"

"Oh, um..." I caught Jonathan eyeing me for just a moment before he slipped his mask back on and turned his attention back to his food. "Dad and I sort of had a fight. I ended up...staying home."

"You were alone on Christmas too? What did you and your father fight about?" Motherly concern was etched across her features, and I loved her for it. She and my dad's divorce had been mostly amicable, but she'd never liked how hard he'd pushed me growing up.

"Just the usual stuff. He asked me when I was going to get a real job and use my degree." I shrugged and shoved a bite of potatoes into my mouth. I couldn't say that it didn't hurt that I didn't have my dad's support, but I could either let it eat at me or I could try to move past it. Jonathan had helped me see that a degree wasn't everything and maybe it was time to pursue what *I* wanted.

"What is it that you do again?" Jon asked, his voice gruff.

"He's a server at Olive & Vine. You know that," my mom responded, shaking her head at him. Jon grumbled in acknowledgment but didn't respond any further.

"Lu—". My eyes shot to Jonathan's, wide with alarm. "Er, can you pass the rolls, Jonathan?"

Our parents continued to eat, my slip going unnoticed, while Jonathan passed me the rolls, shooting me a glare.

Great.

"Well, I just hate the thought that you both spent Christmas alone. If I'd known that was going to be the case, I would have canceled our trip."

"Nonsense. It was nonrefundable. They're grown men. They can manage."

I set my fork down, looking from Jon to Mom to Jonathan. Jon continued to eat, completely unaware of the looks he was receiving from the rest of us. Mom spoke first, addressing her husband from across the table. "Well, that's quite the attitude you have. They're our *family*. They shouldn't be alone at the holidays."

To my surprise, Jonathan chimed in. "It's alright, Suzanne. Dad's always been oblivious to other people's feelings."

Suzanne gasped, and I winced, but before anyone could say anything more, Jon set his fork down with a clack and turned his heated gaze toward Jonathan. "What the hell are you talking about 'feelings?' I gave you everything you needed. *Feelings* don't pay the bills. They don't pay a mort-gage. They don't pay tuition."

Lucy dropped his fork, the two of them squaring off with

full heads of steam while Mom and I gaped at them, our meals entirely forgotten.

"Sure, you provided me a house, but it never felt like a home. You paid for my schooling, but you offered little support when I needed help with my homework. Clothes, a car, school supplies, sports fees...you never failed to support me financially. You even attended awards ceremonies and baseball games. I'm sure you felt that was enough. And it's more than some kids get, but, Dad...I needed more."

There was a lump in my throat and an ache in my heart. Jon hadn't been a bad father. He'd raised Jonathan by himself, which I was sure had been hard as hell. But every kid needs to know they're loved, and Jon had forgotten that part. Now, Jonathan was laying it out there, and I wanted so badly to reach out and offer comfort. Hold his hand. An arm around his shoulder. Something to let him know I had his back. But they didn't know about us, and now didn't seem like the time to shove it in their faces.

"More? I worked my ass off to provide for you. I rearranged my work schedule to get to your games. Called on neighbors to help with transportation. I was a single parent for most of your life. What more did you want from me?"

"Love, Dad. I needed your love. I appreciate all those things you did for me, and I'm sure it wasn't easy, but you never told me you loved me. That you were proud of me. That I'd done a good job." A single tear trailed down Lucy's face, and I couldn't take it anymore. I tossed my napkin next to my plate and rose from the table, walking around to stand behind him with my hand on his shoulder. I was so fucking proud of him, but it tore me apart to see him like this. This had to be so hard for him. But here he was, speaking his truth. It had been a long time coming.

"What are you talking about? Of course I love you. I'm your father." Jon was leaning back in his seat, arms crossed in a defensive posture.

"You never once told me. Not once." Lucy's voice shook with emotion. "I've spent my entire life trying to gain your approval. To make you proud. And not once did you ever tell me how you felt." He scoffed. "Unless it was to tell me how I'd disappointed you. You sure as shit had no problem vocalizing that."

"That's enough. Enough of the antics. Maybe I was tough on you growing up, but that's a father's job. To make sure his son grows up to be a contributing member of society. To keep you in line and on the right path. You didn't need all that lovey-dovey bullshit. You needed guidance and discipline."

"Jesus, Dad. Do you hear yourself? It's not the 1950s, and I'm not a robot. Humans need love. Your *son* needed...needs love." He turned to address my mom. "Suzanne, it was a lovely meal, and I do apologize, but I need to leave. I can't...I just can't be here right now."

I stepped back, dropping my hand from his shoulder and giving him space to stand. He turned toward me, our eyes locking for a moment, and I thought he might say something, but he backed away, disconnecting, and walked through the kitchen. My heart was in my stomach as I watched him go, and I startled when I felt my mom come up behind me, resting her hand on my shoulder, just as I'd done with Jonathan.

"You're in love with him, aren't you?"

I didn't hesitate. "Yes."

"You can tell us how it happened later. Right now, I think he needs you."

"What about...?" I glanced toward Jon, but his seat was empty. I hadn't even heard him exit.

"Don't worry about him. I'll talk to him. He loves Jonathan. Both of you, actually." I wasn't really sure what to do with that. I'd always had an impersonal relationship with Jon because I'd been in high school when they'd gotten married. I'd really only lived with him for a couple of years before going off to college. Mom continued, "He's just never been very good at expressing it."

I turned and hugged her tight, so grateful to have her as my mom. I'd never doubted her love for me. "Love you, Mom."

"Love you too, baby. Now go. We'll talk more later."

25

———

JONATHAN

I swirled the bourbon in my glass, watching the amber liquid wash over the oversized ice cube, coating the inside of the glass before sliding back down to pool at the bottom.

A week ago, almost exactly to the hour, I'd been contemplating a similar glass of bourbon. Amazing what a difference a week could make.

This time, however, I wasn't drunk when the door burst open and Hayden walked back into my life once again. I hadn't been in love with him a week ago. Had barely even scratched the surface of him. And here I was, one week later, totally gone for him, and yet...

And yet.

He'd said he was having second thoughts. But he'd also stood behind me in support, in front of our parents, when I'd unleashed thirty-two years of emotional neglect on my dad in one of the hardest conversations of my life. There were so many mixed signals. I had to think there was more to the story. If I'd learned anything this week, it was to stop jumping to conclusions.

I sipped my bourbon as Hayden approached, vowing to hear him out. The fact that he'd come here had to be a good sign, right?

"My mom knows about us." My eyebrows climbed my forehead as he sunk onto the couch beside me. Those were not the words I'd expected to come out of his mouth. "Right after you left, she asked me if I was in love with you."

I swallowed hard, my heart climbing up into my throat. "What did you say?"

He turned toward me, running his hand through my beard, then cupping the back of my neck. I fucking loved it when he did that.

"I said yes."

"Really?"

His fingers dug into the nape of my neck as he chewed on his lip and nodded his head twice.

A slow smile spread across my face, joy radiating through my body as I lunged at him, sloshing bourbon everywhere in my haste to wrap my arms around him. "Shit. Sorry." I set the glass down on the coffee table and then swiped at him with my bare hands, but Hayden pushed them away in favor of pulling me into a hug.

"What I said on the porch—right as my mom opened the door—I was trying to tell you I didn't want to keep us a secret anymore. I was having second thoughts about *that,* not us."

"I thought maybe you were going to call the whole thing off. But the more I thought about it once I got home, the more I realized that didn't make sense. You wouldn't have called it off and then stood by me like you did with my dad." I pulled back to look at him. "Thanks for that, by the way. For standing behind me like you did. It gave me the strength to say what I needed to say."

"You don't have to thank me, Lucy. I've always got your back." He kissed me tenderly, just a brush of his lips against mine. "I was so damn proud of you."

"Oh. Um, thanks. I want to say that it felt good to get all that off my chest, but it really didn't. It felt awful." I let out a breath, running my hand through my hair. "Don't get me wrong, it needed to be said, and I'm glad I did, but that doesn't mean it felt good. My dad really did do a lot for me growing up, and I do appreciate it. I don't want him to think I don't. I don't want him to think I'm selfish."

"You're not selfish, Lucy. But feelings and relationships are complicated. You can feel appreciative in some ways and neglected in others. Both can be true. And owning your feelings, calling him out on all the ways he fell short, isn't selfish. I think you were damn brave for doing it."

I leaned forward again, pressing my forehead to his and breathing him in. I wasn't sure what I'd done to deserve him, but I would spend the rest of my life doing my damndest to keep him. No one had ever made me feel as good as he did. The fact that he loved me was a fucking miracle.

"Hay?"

"Yeah?"

I brushed his hair back off his face, looking into those chocolate pools I could spend hours getting lost in. "I love you too."

He smiled wide, my golden retriever of a boyfriend lighting up from the inside out. He popped off the couch, grabbed my hand, and pulled me up. I'd barely gotten my feet under me when he began tugging me down the hall.

"Where are we going?"

"To bed. You're going to show me how much."

My brow creased in confusion. "How much, what?"

He looked at me over his shoulder, pausing at the door

to my bedroom. "How much you love me." He winked and pulled me through the door.

26

HAYDEN

December 31

Inspired by Lucy's confrontation with Jon last night, I'd texted my dad and asked if I could stop by the house this afternoon. I was nervous but also, strangely, excited. For the first time in my life, I had direction. I had a goal I'd set my sights on, something that was for me and not anyone else. It was time I started creating a life that I could be proud of. Something that excited me and set fire to my soul. I hoped my father could support me, but if not...well, we'd cross that bridge when we came to it.

I knocked on the door, shivering in the December chill. Lucy had wanted to come with me, to be a support in the same way I had been for him, but I'd decided that shoving my relationship with my stepbrother in my father's face at the same time I was telling him I was pursuing a music career, might be a lot for him to take.

The door swung open, and I was greeted by my thirteen-year-old half-sister. She barely looked up from her phone as she stood back to allow me to enter. "Dad's back in his office," she said without looking up.

"Thanks, brat," I said as I ruffled her hair.

"Hey!" she called out as I walked away.

I made my way to Dad's office, knocking lightly on the open door before crossing the threshold into the room. He looked up from his computer, offering me a distracted smile. "Hey. Have a seat. I just need to finish up this email."

Too nervous to sit, I opted to stay standing, instead crossing over to the bookshelf to look at the framed photographs mixed in among books and other knick-knacks my stepmother no doubt had a hand in choosing.

"Hayden! It's so good to see you!" Jessica, my stepmom, appeared in the open doorway, a basket of laundry on her hip, her long auburn hair in a single braid down her back. I walked over and hugged her. Even one-handed, she gave the best hugs. "Can I get you anything to drink?"

"Oh, no thanks, I'm good."

"Well, I'll leave you to it. Don't be a stranger, okay?" She leaned to the right, peering around me at my father with brows raised in warning. "And you...be good, yeah?"

"I'm always good."

"I'm serious. Listen to what he has to say. Be open-minded. I happen to like my stepson and don't want him to become a stranger in this house because his father is too stubborn to listen."

God, Jessica was great. I was so lucky to have a great mom and stepmom in my life.

"Yes, dear," my father responded, but there was a smile on his face, and I knew he'd at least try to take her words to heart.

Jessica rolled her eyes, kissed my cheek, and then left me and my father alone again.

This time, I did take a seat, wanting to be at eye level with him. "I wanted to talk to you about the fight we had before Christmas. More specifically, the topic of the fight."

"Okay. I'm listening."

I blew out a breath. I was twenty-four. Had been on my own for a while now. Why was this so hard?

"I know you want me to use my degree, but I've decided to pursue a career in music. Or at least, I want to try it. I'm going to keep my job at Olive & Vine. I've already spoken to my manager. He's willing to work with me on giving me nights off when I have gigs, as long as I give him plenty of notice, but I'll still be able to work plenty of shifts so I can pay the bills like I do now."

"What kind of music gigs?" His expression and tone of voice were neutral. I couldn't get a feel for what he was thinking, but I took the fact he hadn't dismissed the whole idea out of turn as a good sign.

"I'm still figuring that out, honestly. I play and sing a lot of styles, so I'm still deciding what my niche might be. And I'm going to start lessons again. On both guitar and voice. My old guitar teacher has an opening starting in February, and he recommended a voice instructor who I'm meeting with next week."

"So, you're pretty serious about this then?"

"Yeah, Dad, I am. I've been thinking about this for a long time, but I knew you wanted me to use my degree, so I never pursued it. And I—"

"Hayden, did you ever apply or interview for a single job in the business sector?"

Here it comes.

"No, I—"

"Then what's the real reason you never pursued music? Because you never pursued a job that would have actually used your degree either. I would have supported you on the music thing."

"You...what?"

"I just wanted you to find your direction. To do something meaningful with your life. Business made the most sense because it gives you a lot of options, but if you'd told me you wanted to pursue music, I would have supported that. You've always been talented."

I was gobsmacked. Completely at a loss for words.

As my mouth hung open, he rose, coming out from behind his desk to lean on the front of it and face me.

"Look, I know I've been hard on you. But that's because I knew you were meant for more in this life. You've always been smart, but working as a server for the rest of your life —you could do so much more."

"There's nothing wrong with being a server."

"No, there's not. But do you still want to be waiting tables when you're fifty-three? Seventy-two? With no health plan and no retirement?"

"Honestly, Dad, I don't have those answers. And I don't know what will come out of this music thing, but I have to try it. It's the only thing I've ever been passionate about, and I want to see where it takes me."

"So why didn't you pursue it sooner? It isn't because you were afraid of what I'd say. If you were really worried about seeking my approval, you would have gotten a job in business a long time ago. Instead, you fought me every time I brought it up. So you clearly weren't worried about pissing me off. What's the real reason?"

Goddammit. He knew me better than I realized.

"I...I guess I was scared."

"Of what?"

My heart was racing, thumping violently in my chest, as

he forced me to expose my biggest fear. Because he was right. If pleasing him had really been my concern, I would have gotten a job in business a long time ago.

"I'm scared I'll fail at the only thing I've ever really cared about doing."

"Then *that's* why you should go for it." He smiled wide. "You've found something worth taking a risk for."

"Aren't you supposed to tell me about all the ways I'm going to fail? And how music isn't a stable career? You already mentioned the retirement thing," I grumbled.

He chuckled. "I'm not going to tell you that I won't worry about this path you're choosing, but that isn't to say we can't work through some of those obstacles. I can get you a meeting with my financial adviser. He can get you set up with some accounts for retirement or at least steer you in the right direction. And you're right, music isn't a stable career." He sat next to me on the loveseat, angling in my direction. "But this is the first time I've ever seen you passionate enough about something to confront me about it. To come to me with a plan, ready to lay it all on the line. I'm proud of you."

I swallowed past the lump that had developed in my throat, trying to find my voice. This conversation was not going as I'd expected. I'd been so ready to defend myself that it hadn't occurred to me that he might be supportive. It was amazing, but without that need to defend myself, I was left feeling vulnerable. "I'm scared, Dad."

"Of course you are." He smacked me on the arm playfully. "Welcome to adulting."

I huffed out a laugh. "Gee, thanks."

"You're welcome," he said, his voice overly cheerful.

"I, um, have a gig tonight if you want to come?" Shit. I

hadn't meant to invite him. I wasn't sure I was ready for that yet.

"Yeah? I'd love to. I'll talk to Jess."

"I mean, it's okay if you don't make it. It's not a big deal if you have plans for New Year's and all."

His smile stretched from ear to ear. "We wouldn't miss it."

27

JONATHAN

Hayden was nervous as fuck.

We were at a small music club, and Hayden was set to go on in about ten minutes. The person who'd been originally scheduled to play the special engagement for the club's New Year's Eve bash had tested positive for Covid. I wasn't clear on how the club had gotten Hayden's name, but as far as I could tell, it was a friend-of-a-friend connection of some sort that had led to the call.

We'd arrived about twenty minutes ago, having already gone through a sound check earlier this afternoon. Since we'd arrived this evening, he'd tuned his guitar, checked the mics, used the restroom, and had nearly worn a path in the carpet backstage.

"Here." I handed him a shot glass filled with vodka, keeping a larger glass of bourbon for myself. I planned to sip mine, but I hoped the shot might help him take the edge off. He downed it, then handed it back to me. "Thanks."

"You're going to be fine. I'll stand in the back, and you can sing every song to me, just like you did at the cabin."

"I was nervous there too."

193

I laughed, then pulled Hayden into me, setting my bourbon aside on a nearby table so I could wrap my arms around him. "Baby, I love you. You're going to be great. And when you're done, we'll go back to my house and have our own celebration to ring in the new year."

"What kind of celebration do you have in mind?"

I chuckled against his neck. "Well, let's see...I figured we'd definitely be naked, and I've got champagne chilling in the fridge."

"What if I don't want you completely naked?"

"Oh yeah?"

Hayden leaned back and ran his fingers along the buttons of my vest. "I think I might like you to keep the vest on."

"Just the vest?"

"Yep. You're so fucking sexy in this thing." Because it was a fancy New Year's Eve bash that the club was hosting, we were both dressed up. I'd chosen a three-piece suit in charcoal, knowing the cut of the pants showed off my ass particularly well. Hayden and I had needed to make an emergency trip to purchase a suit for him and had been lucky to find a store that was open and could make necessary alterations on such short notice, considering it was a holiday. He looked damn fine in his black suit and black dress shirt underneath. The only pop of color came from his tie, which was gold silk.

The stage manager popped his head back, letting us know Hayden had five minutes until showtime.

"I'm going to head out front and find a spot. You're going to be amazing." I kissed him deeply, then grabbed my bourbon and turned to make my way out to the front of the house.

"Wait." I turned, eyebrows raised in question. He

stepped forward so we were just a few inches apart. "I just wanted to say thank you. For believing in me, pushing me, and supporting me. I never would have taken this gig if it weren't for you."

"Ah, Hay. That's sweet. But if not this gig, there would have been another one. I think you were always meant to do this."

"Maybe. But I still appreciate the nudge."

"Anytime, baby. You got this!"

My boyfriend was killing it on stage, and I'd be lying if I said it wasn't a total turn-on watching him do his thing. Despite the nerves I'd seen him exhibit backstage, he'd performed his first set with complete confidence, as if he'd been doing this for years. When he'd taken a quick break between sets, it had taken all my self-control not to haul him into the back and bend him over the couch I'd seen earlier in the green room.

He was midway through his second set when I spotted Suzanne and my father making their way through the crowd to the standing cocktail table I'd snagged in the back near the bar. My father made a beeline for the bar while Suzanne came over and greeted me warmly with a hug. There wasn't an opportunity for conversation, as we were engrossed in watching Hayden perform, so we stood side by side, swaying to the music. My father approached with a cocktail for Suzanne and what I assumed was a bourbon for himself, taking up position on Suzanne's other side.

My blood hummed with anxiety, replaying the words we'd thrown at each other last night and wondering what we might say to each other now. Whatever might be said, I didn't want to ruin Hayden's big night. I silently vowed to keep it civil for his sake.

Shortly after the arrival of Suzanne and my father, Hayden's dad, Mark, and stepmother, Jessica, arrived, crowding in at our tiny table. From what I understood, the divorce between Hayden's parents had been mostly amicable, and I was glad, for his sake, that all parties seemed to get along.

We all watched, beaming, as Hayden sang, strumming the guitar with precision as he belted out a cover of a Dave Matthews Band song. The crowd was pressed up to the stage, hands waving in the air, as they sang about playing under the table and dreaming. I stood in awe at the magnificence of him, eyes closed, singing an iconic song like a boss. Like this was what he'd been made to do. I couldn't have been prouder.

I felt a tap on my shoulder and turned, surprised to find myself looking into the eyes of my father. He nodded toward the hallway leading to the restrooms, but I shook my head. This was Hayden's night, not the time for this conversation.

He pressed his face next to mine, speaking into my ear. "Just hear me out." I started to shake my head, but he cut me off, surprising me with, "Please."

I huffed but jerked a nod and made to follow him, hoping Hayden wouldn't notice my absence. I wanted him focused on his performance, not distracted with worry over my father and me.

We found our way into the hallway leading to the restrooms and leaned against the wall, facing each other. The music was muted back here, no longer drowning out the hammering of my own pulse.

"Suzanne wanted me to talk to you—"

"Oh, *Suzanne* did, huh?"

"She thought I should apologize for the way I spoke to you last night."

"Oh, she did, did she?" I knew I was being a bit petulant as I crossed my arms, but I wasn't willing to let him off the hook. If he was going to apologize to me, he needed to own it.

He sighed, then crossed his arms, mirroring my stance. "Have you made your point?"

"You tell me. If we're only having this conversation so you can get back in Suzanne's good graces, then we might as well go back out there now. This is Hayden's night."

His face flushed, but when he didn't say anything further, I turned to walk away. His hand on my arm stopped me.

"I'm sorry." I turned, nodding at him to continue. "I've never been good at expressing myself emotionally."

I snorted. That was a massive understatement.

He glared at me but continued, "When your mom passed, I was lost. She was the only one who could get me to say the things I'd never said to anyone else. And the pain of losing her...it was unbearable." He scrubbed a hand over his face, and my anger began to dissipate, sympathy taking its place. "Like I said, I was never good at the emotional stuff, but after your mom...I just sort of locked it down. It was too hard. I had you to take care of, and I just sort of went into survival mode."

"Dad, I—"

"Just let me get this out." I nodded again, swallowing past the lump in my throat. "I'm proud of you. Always have been. You're smart. You work hard. Have a good head on your shoulders." If he noticed the shine in my eyes, he didn't comment on it. "I was hard on you growing up because I was trying to compensate for you only having one parent. I wanted to make sure you were going to be a good person who could thrive and be successful." He paused, looking down at his feet before looking back at me once again. "I guess I forgot to make sure you understood that I love you and I'm proud of you too."

"I love you too, Dad," I whispered, choking back the tears threatening to fall.

"I'm sorry, son. I'm probably never going to be the type of guy who wears his heart on his sleeve, but I'll try to remember to say something more often to...you know...let you know how I feel."

I chuckled. I couldn't help it. He was clearly so uncomfortable with all of this, but he was trying, and that meant the world to me.

I wanted to hug him, but I thought that might be pushing it for tonight, so I settled for putting my hand on his shoulder and giving it a squeeze.

"You gave me a great childhood, Dad. You supported me. Came to all my piano recitals and baseball games. Paid for my college. I don't want you to think I don't appreciate that."

"I know you do."

"Hey, you two." I turned to see Suzanne striding toward us, a look of concern on her face. "You've been gone for a while. Everything okay?"

I smiled at her. "Yeah. We're good." Her eyes flicked back and forth between the two of us as if trying to determine whether I was telling the truth.

"Well, if you're finished, you should probably get back out there. Hayden keeps looking over at our corner like he's looking for you. And there's only about ten minutes 'til midnight."

We followed her back out just as Hayden was finishing a cover of "Semi-Charmed Life" by Third Eye Blind, and I thought he might have a future covering nineties alternative and grunge. He caught my eye, raising an eyebrow in question, and I smiled, letting him know everything was okay.

Moments later, the manager of the club took over the mic to hand it off to a local celebrity who was going to do the official countdown to midnight. Complementary champagne was distributed by the waitstaff as Hayden made his way back to our corner near the bar. He'd still have another hour or so to play after midnight, but at least he had a short break to come say hi and ring in the new year with us.

"Hey."

"Hey," I said and kissed him, right there in front of our families.

"You're supposed to wait until midnight," he said when we pulled apart.

"I missed you."

He laughed. "We're in the same room."

"Yeah, but I can't kiss you and touch you when you're on stage."

"True, but—"

"Nine, eight, seven..." All around us, the club was filled with people happily counting down with their friends and loved ones around them. Arms wrapped around each other. I looked into Hayden's eyes, the two of us counting down together, and I marveled at how much brighter my life was now that Hayden was in it.

Over the years, I hadn't given a lot of thought to New Year's resolutions. The new year had simply been a marker for the passage of time from one year to the next. But this year, for the first time, I set one. I vowed to love deeper and laugh often. And to spend as much time wrapped up in Hayden as I could.

"Three...two...one!"

I dove in and kissed him, keeping it relatively chaste in the midst of the crowd and our families.

"I love you," I whispered against his lips.

"I love you more."

The End

EPILOGUE
HAYDEN

February 14

I'd barely seen my boyfriend in the last couple of weeks, and the need I had for him was a physical ache. He grounded me. Quieted the chaos in my mind without making me feel bad and without trying to change who I was. I wouldn't have guessed it before we ventured into this relationship, but he was a caretaker. It was as if I'd unlocked something inside him, a need to help me, support me, encourage me.

Love me.

I'd once thought he was stuffy and cold. Judgmental. Rigid. But the man I'd fallen in love with just a couple of months ago was none of those things. With me, he was warm, understanding, and patient. He still liked order and routine and valued cleanliness, timeliness, and predictability, but those were strengths in his personality, and frankly, they were my guardrails when I started to careen off track.

I'd started to learn to embrace my ADHD and the ways it made me a more well-rounded person and a stronger musician. I still struggled with time management and being easily distracted. I was messy, disorganized, and forgetful. But my Lucy helped me get back on track. He reminded me to set alarms on my phone when I needed to remember something really important. He DoorDashed me food when I forgot to eat because I was hyperfocused on writing a new piece of music. And I'd gotten a lot better about keeping my apartment clean because I knew it made him happy. And for all the ways he made my life better, I wanted to return those things in equal measure.

I wanted to say he made me a better man, and that was true, but I thought maybe I did the same for him. And in that way, we were a perfect match.

If only we could find more time to spend together.

I walked in through the garage, treading softly due to the late hour. It was after midnight on a Monday, so it was quite possible he was asleep, though with it being Valentine's Day, he might have tried to wait up. Still, I moved quietly, just to be safe.

I grabbed two forks from the kitchen and made my way into the living room, where a single lamp was shining next to the leather couch. Jonathan, bless him, was stretched out in his pajama pants, blanket half tossed over his legs, hands resting on his bare chest, fast asleep.

I set the takeout container and forks on the coffee table and knelt on the floor near his head, taking a moment to study him as he slept. After coming home from the cabin, he'd kept the beard, mostly because I'd threatened to leave him if he shaved it off. We both knew that was bullshit, but he'd kept it anyway because he liked to make me happy.

And I liked the way his beard felt against my thighs.

He kept the beard neat and tidy, of course, but that didn't stop me from running my hands through his whiskers, savoring the feel of him against my skin. On an inhale, he nuzzled into my hand, making a contented sound, then lazily opened his eyes.

"Hey, you," he said, his voice raspy from sleep. "What time is it?"

I looked at the clock on the mantel. "Twelve-fifteen. Sorry I woke you." I bent and pressed my lips to his, lingering there a moment before pulling back.

"It's okay. I wanted to see you."

"Mmm." I rubbed his nose with mine. "I wanted to see you too." Unable to help myself, I laid my head on his chest, listening to the steady beat of his heart. The sound and feel of it soothed my soul in a way nothing else could.

"How was your day?" His voice rumbled in his chest underneath my ear.

"Good. Exhausting, but good." I'd worked the lunch shift at Olive & Vine so I could take a gig in the evening. Word had gotten around after my New Year's Eve performance, and I'd been steadily playing in clubs and coffee houses ever since. Tonight's gig had been a fun one, playing at the same club as I'd played on New Year's Eve. It had been an anti-Valentine gig, and despite being hopelessly in love with my own Valentine, I'd had a blast playing breakup anthems for the single set.

Lucy stifled a yawn, and I sat up. "I brought you some leftover chocolate cake from Olive & Vine. You want some?"

"Now?"

"Sure. Why not?"

"It's so late." Oh, sweet Lucy. Always a stickler for the rules.

"Eh. We're grown-ups. We can eat cake whenever we want." I shot him a shit-eating grin, and he sat up, making room for me on the couch. I plopped down next to him and swung one of my legs over his, then fed him a bite of the decadent dessert. The sound he made went straight to my groin. "Moan like that again, and I'm going to have to skip this dessert in favor of something even better."

"Is that a threat or a promise?" His eyes twinkled as he fed me a bite, and I moaned in pleasure. This was damn good cake.

"It's whatever you want it to be, babe."

He leaned over and kissed me, the chocolate and raspberry flavor on his tongue tangling with mine. Before long, the kiss turned desperate, the cake forgotten in favor of tasting each other instead.

I pulled away, grabbed his fork, set it alongside mine inside the plastic container, and returned it to the coffee table. Cake out of the way, I climbed onto his lap, straddling his hips and grinding my erection into his while I licked a stripe from his ear down the column of his throat, then nibbled the hollow of his shoulder.

Things progressed quickly from there. Shoes were removed, and clothes were discarded—including my red heart briefs—as we hastily undressed each other in the middle of his living room. It had been two weeks since I'd had him inside me, and I was desperate for that unique sense of connection I only felt when he was buried balls deep, with eyes locked on mine, hips thrusting and grinding against me, while he took me apart, piece by piece.

I wanted that more than I wanted my next breath.

Hands and tongues roamed as we reacquainted ourselves with each other's bodies. Two weeks might as well have been two years with the frantic way we nipped and bit and clawed at each other.

Somehow, we ended up on the floor with me straddling

Lucy's hips, our dicks leaking and making a mess between us as we kissed hungrily.

"Do you have lube down here?" I asked between kisses.

"I may have put some in the media cabinet after the last time we messed around down here."

I retrieved the bottle and climbed back on top of him in record time. "Never in my life did I think I'd find being prepared so fucking hot. You're a goddamn Boy Scout, Lucy."

"I thought *you* were the Boy Scout of sex supplies?"

"Mmm." I kissed him deeply. "We can both claim the title."

He hissed as I poured an excessive amount of the cool liquid on his erection, overdoing it in my haste and making a mess. I swiped some of the excess lube and began working myself open, too impatient to let him do it for me.

"Slow down, Hay. I took tomorrow off. We have all night."

"Can't. Want you too much." Deciding I was ready enough, I leaned forward, lining up his cock with my entrance, and slid down his length until he was fully seated inside me.

"*Fuuuck,* you feel good, baby." His hands gripped my hips, holding me in place as tremors of ecstasy washed through both of us.

Home.

The feeling of him buried so deep was like coming home, and something settled inside me. It was peace and comfort and joy and love. I'd never stop chasing this feeling for as long as I lived.

He rocked his hips, urging me to move, and I obliged, sliding up and down his length, picking up the pace, until we were a blur of movement. The sound of our bodies slapping over and over was obscene, and the muscles in my thighs and hamstrings screamed as I pushed myself faster and harder, chasing both our orgasms.

I leaned over, bracing my hands on the floor next to his shoulders, changing the angle and trapping my dick between us, then continued our frantic pace. Grunts and groans added to the soundtrack of our lovemaking as this new angle gave my dick the delicious friction it had been missing, and he pegged my prostate over and over.

Balls drawn up tight, knowing I was about to blow, I took his mouth in mine, wanting to be as connected as possible when our orgasms detonated. Moments later, he tensed inside me, thrusting with his hips and painting my insides with his release. My own orgasm followed, spreading in sticky spurts between us. We muttered and mumbled, our words incoherent and nonsensical as the aftershocks rolled through us until my arms finally gave out and I collapsed on top of him in a sweaty, sticky mess. As far as I was concerned, I never wanted to move from this spot ever again. My body had become jello.

"Mmm, I've missed that," I said in his ear, still trying to catch my breath.

"Move in with me."

I found the strength to pull my head up enough to look at him. "What did you say?"

"I said, move in with me." The bastard dropped that bomb on me and didn't even bother to open his eyes.

"Are you serious?"

He did open his eyes then. "Yeah. You said you missed this. Move in with me. I know our schedules are challenging, but if you live with me, I get you in my bed every night. I get to kiss you in the morning before I go to work. You'll kiss me at night when you come home. I want you here. You belong here with me."

By the time he finished his little speech, I was grinning from ear to ear. I could picture it—had already pictured it—a life with him. And now that he'd said it aloud, I wanted it with a ferocity that surprised me with its intensity.

"Yes. Absolutely, yes." I peppered him with kisses all over his face, repeating yes between each one. He laughed and grabbed the sides of my face, stopping my attack and forcing me to look him in the eye.

"I love you, Hayden. Happy Valentine's Day."

"I love you too, Lucy. So fucking much."

THE END

Want more Jonathan and Hayden? Click here for a Bonus Epilogue!

Want to interact with me and other readers to discuss the book, learn more about my inspiration, and see what I'm working on next? Join my readers group on facebook: Melody's Lane.

ALSO BY MELODY CLAIRE

When He Saved Me

Jamie & Finn

My emotional new adult romance featuring a broody barista and a sunshiney college student navigating love and loss. It's a standalone and comes with a guaranteed HEA.

Content Warnings can be found at https://melodyclaireauthor.com/ trigger-warnings/.

AUTHOR'S NOTE

I wrote this book in just two months in the busiest part of my year. I had an idea I couldn't let go of and after debating whether I was crazy, I decided to run with it! It was intense, but I'm so pleased with how it turned out!

Jonathan and Hayden were so much fun to write! I loved the dichotomy of having a character with ADHD who feels a little misunderstood, while also being unapologetically himself. And sweet Jonathan being completely baffled by someone who might dare to see the world through a different lens. It was fun to see him evolve throughout the story.

A note about writing a character with ADHD...I have witnessed countless students with ADHD come through my classroom over the years. I drew on my experiences watching those kiddos tackle the various challenges it presents in their lives to create Hayden's character. Having said that, each person's experience and relationship with ADHD is different. Additionally, I had two different sensitivity readers provide feedback, and they each had different thoughts on it as well. All of this to say, Hayden's character is just one presentation of what ADHD might look like. There are many other ways it might take shape in you or someone you know. Ultimately, it was important to me that Hayden's experiences felt realistic, and not like a cartoon version written in for a punchline. Hopefully I did him justice.

ACKNOWLEDGMENTS

I wrote another book! It wouldn't have been possible without the help of a village of amazing people.

To my husband - I don't know if I will ever be able to express how much your support of me embarking on this writing journey has meant to me. I am so lucky to have my very own book boyfriend.

To my girls - You are my why.

To Kayla, Aiden, Nicole, Francesca, and Charlotte - your feedback was spot on as usual. Thank you for making sure Jonathan and Hayden were the best versions of themselves they could be!

To Abbie - Thank you for polishing my words and for answering my random grammatical questions at all hours of the day!

To Amanda - I'm so thankful for your friendship! For pushing me and talking me off of ledges and everything in between, your support is immeasurable!

ABOUT THE AUTHOR

Melody Claire writes emotional contemporary MM romance stories with moderate heat and a whole lot of heart. She hails from Kansas City but resides in Omaha and loves setting her stories in the Midwest. She is married with two almost grown kiddos, a dog, and a kitty. By day, she teaches middle school, and by night can be found writing on her laptop or curled up with her kindle. She's addicted to Pink Drinks and the sound of her husband's laugh, and loves nothing more than to escape into a love story.

Connect With Me!

www.ingramcontent.com/pod-product-compliance
Lightning Source LLC
Chambersburg PA
CBHW020913160726
47993CB00005B/1953